Pistolero

Paul Bedford

A Black Horse Western

ROBERT HALE · LONDON

© Paul Bedford 2014
First published in Great Britain 2014

ISBN 978-0-7198-1409-9

Robert Hale Limited
Clerkenwell House
Clerkenwell Green
London EC1R 0HT

www.halebooks.com

Typeset by
Derek Doyle & Associates, Shaw Heath
Printed and bound in Great Britain by
CPI Antony Rowe, Chippenham and Eastbourne

Pistolero

In the summer of 1872 a deadly pistolero, Brett Dalton, is hired to assassinate President Ulysses S. Grant as he embarks on a re-election campaign across the western states. The President will be travelling via the Union Pacific Railroad, and when his locomotive stops to take on water at an isolated pumping station on the Nebraska/Wyoming border the lethal plot will be launched.

With hostile Sioux Indians also planning to attack the train, it is up to Thaddeus McEvoy, a special investigator in the newly formed Department of Justice, to save Grant's life. Widower Tatum Barklam and his beautiful daughter, Sarah, are used to a predictable life at the pumping station, but they are about to experience a very different pace when Dalton and his gang of desperadoes come thundering into their lives.

CHAPTER ONE

Senator Augustus J. Breckenridge was one of two men elected to the US Senate by the good people of Minnesota. He had achieved such eminence by dint of his undistinguished but greatly exaggerated war service with the Union forces. He was a blowhard and a braggart, with an inflated opinion of his own worth. His strong views against the defeated South had inevitably brought him to the attention of those who sought retribution upon the victorious North *and* were about to bring about the senator's death.

The lean, compactly built individual strode through the grand entrance of the State Capitol building in St Paul and moved purposefully towards the magnificent staircase. There was something about his physique and the determined set to his features that drew more than one second glance, but nobody would have considered demanding to know his business. Although quite obviously a man of the West, the stranger carried no visible weapons and his sombre dark suit was clearly expensive and well brushed. As he mounted the stairs two at a time, his piercing eyes searched for anyone or anything that could possibly pose a threat.

Reaching the first floor, he paused momentarily as though getting his bearings. He knew exactly where he was going, but took the time to check his 'back trail'. Satisfied that all was well, he advanced on a set of imposing double doors. Amazingly there was not even a secretary of any kind on hand to enquire as to his presence there. The knife scabbard nestled comfortingly in the small of his back as he reached out to the highly polished wooden door handle.

It was immediately obvious that Gus Breckenridge was not expecting visitors. As his killer entered the vast room, the senator was poised in front of a mirror. He had just inserted a small pair of scissors into his left nostril, with a view to trimming the unruly hairs that sprouted there. At the sight of a total stranger in his midst, his naturally short temper flared up.

'Who the devil are you? Get the hell out of here before I have you thrown out.'

The unwelcome visitor merely favoured him with a mirthless smile and closed the door. Then, suddenly moving at great speed, he advanced across the room towards its outraged occupant. That anger abruptly turned to fear as recognition dawned on the politician that here was not just some local come to lobby a state official. The interloper possessed a lean muscularity and menacing demeanour that had Breckenridge reaching for his stout walking stick.

Even as his assailant's hand grasped the knife under his jacket, that man recognized the poetic justice that presented itself and abruptly changed his mind. Instead, he bunched his fist and slammed it squarely into his victim's face. As blood gushed from his broken nose, Breckenridge rocked back on his heels in shock, all thought of resistance forgotten. The resolutely silent stranger ducked to the side and seized the heavily weighted stick.

Violent assaults on members of Congress were not unheard of and the choice of weapon appealed to his twisted sense of humour. Stepping back, he swung the club at the disorientated senator with unerring accuracy. The weighted handle smashed into the side of his skull with sickening force. With a strangled cry, he fell heavily to the floor. The assassin peered down at him with detached and professional interest as a pool of blood began to spread across the polished wood.

'One more to be certain,' he decided.

Wielding the walking stick like an axe, he brought it down on his defenceless victim's forehead and grunted with satisfaction as Breckenridge's eyes flickered and closed for the last time. Taking care to keep any blood away from his clothes, the deadly interloper casually tossed the weapon on to the body and coolly walked away without a backward glance. He was a full block away before the blood-soaked corpse was discovered. Law enforcement methods in that year of 1872 allowed little chance of discovering his identity.

Silas Beauregard peered intently at the rumpled telegram in his grasp and slowly the makings of a smile spread over his embittered features. The news on the paper was intentionally vague and, due to the deliberately tortuous delivery route, over a day old. That didn't detract from the satisfaction of knowing that another Northern 'butcher' was dead. Nevertheless, his hand shook slightly as he took up his pen and dipped it in the inkpot. He wrote the following:

I take great pleasure in your news STOP I believe it is now time for you to offer my kind regards to Governor Byron Taylforth of Iowa STOP I have it on good authority that he is visiting Council Bluffs towards the end of the month STOP That should give you time to prepare the necessary greeting STOP

Barely had he finished writing before his mind began to wander. The pen fell from his fingers and rolled across the highly polished desk. As on so many occasions, the memories took over and the room around him no longer seemed to exist. The passing of time had not lessened their frightening power and clarity. The huge Georgia mansion reduced to smoking ashes. The extensive fields untended and the valuable slaves scattered to the four winds. Rows of bayonets atop blue uniforms seemed to stretch endlessly before him.

And then, as always, the lifeless body of his beloved wife loomed large. Strangely, he had never been able to picture his only son's demise. Maybe because the possibilities were far too horrifying. He had never believed the sanitized report that had reached him, and any death in the trenches around Petersburg could only have been unspeakably grim.

It was the knowledge that General, and now President, Ulysses S. Grant had overseen that bloody siege that provided the impetus for the seed of an idea that was now growing within him. Grant's desire for re-election, coupled with his proposed journey on the amazing new transcontinental railroad, might just provide someone with the opportunity to avenge his son's death in a most spectacular manner. After all, it wouldn't be the first time that a serving president of the United States had been assassinated!

They say that you should always expect the unexpected, but he had not anticipated encountering a guard.

'Who might you be, sir? State your business.'

The man possessed a strong and authoritative voice. The hard eyes and tied-down gun suggested that he knew his trade. When he did not get an immediate response his hand settled firmly over the butt of the cap-and-ball Remington at his side. It was a rugged, reliable solid-framed revolver, often chosen by professionals. The stranger favoured him with a disarming smile and a comforting drawl.

'Careful with that firearm, mister. Me and the governor are old friends. He's always telling me how he likes to take in the early-morning air, so I thought I'd just mosey on down here and join him.'

The slightest flicker of uncertainty registered with the bodyguard and it was all the edge that the visitor needed. His Colt Navy Sheriff nestled in a belly holster, which allowed for a fast draw even when its owner was mounted. The weapon streaked out of the oiled gun leather with practised ease, ensuring that the luckless gunhand never had a chance. The piece discharged with dispassionate fury, sending a .36 calibre lead ball into and then out of his unprotected skull. Blood and brain matter splashed on to the earth as the now lifeless bodyguard toppled out of the saddle.

As a small cloud of sulphurous smoke blew off on the wind, the stranger pulled away to approach the startled politician. Alarm and disbelief registered on that individual's features in equal proportions. His sudden mood change seemed to infect his horse, because that animal began to restlessly shift position so that its rider struggled to control it. The menacing newcomer approached with his revolver cocked and levelled.

The Governor of Iowa had the silver hair and patrician appearance of one well suited to high office. When visiting the town of Council Bluffs on business, it was his custom to take an early-morning ride on the open ground overlooking the Missouri River. Any pleasure that gave him was certainly not evident now.

'Why?' he croaked dismally.

'The best of all reasons, sir,' replied his assassin. 'Money!'

With that, his finger tightened on the trigger. It was at that instant that the governor's highly strung thoroughbred chose to twist around towards the river. The stranger took a snap decision and lowered his weapon. Taking careful aim, he fired instead at the animal's left flank. The ball gouged a bloody furrow through its soft flesh. With a scream of pain the beast took off blindly towards the riverbank, instinctively trying to escape the source of its suffering. In its demented state it took no account of the fast-approaching watercourse and continued at full pelt. And all the while, its luckless rider desperately struggled to rein it in.

Drawing a bead on the governor's broad back, the shootist waited patiently for him to reach the edge and then fired. The momentum threw the mortally wounded man forward, but he was still in the saddle as both horse and rider plunged into the wide Missouri. The originator of their demise holstered his weapon with a satisfied sigh and urged his own mount carefully over to the riverbank. The stricken politician had already disappeared under the surface, leaving the floundering animal to its own devices.

'I'll bet he really loved that creature,' the stranger muttered. Movement on the other bank of the river caught his eye. Railroad workers from Omaha's engine sheds had witnessed the terrible 'accident' and were hollering vague fragments of advice over to him. With a languid wave, that man calmly turned away and headed back towards Council Bluffs. Nobody was on hand to pursue the brutal killer and a hearty breakfast beckoned. Brett Dalton rode back to town with the unhurried assurance of one who apparently had nothing to fear from the law.

CHAPTER TWO

The two men could quite easily have been salesmen from back East, bringing the latest manufactured marvels to the far-flung frontier. They both wore sober frock-coats and carried carpetbags of a type being made infamous in the South's reconstruction. Their hands were clean and completely lacking the calluses that marked out a manual worker. It could only be on much closer inspection that anyone might question their occupation. There was a hard set to their features that might easily have intimidated potential customers. Their eyes were guarded and watchful, as with the hunter or hunted, which suggested either involvement in law enforcement or criminal activities.

And then there were the weapons. It would be another year before cartridge revolvers were generally available to the public and yet both men carried versions of the Colt Army that no longer required to be painstakingly reloaded from the front. In fact they were chambered to take the same ammunition as that held in the tubular magazines of the Winchester carbines deposited near their feet.

As the Rock Island Railroad carriage rattled and swayed towards its destination, Jud Parker could no longer contain his curiosity.

'Sweet Jesus, Thad. Are you going to tell me the real reason for this trip? How can I back your play if I don't know what we're getting into?'

Thaddeus McEvoy was the taller of the two, possessing a lean muscularity and strength that had caught some men unawares. He viewed his companion in speculative silence from under the brim of his hat. The two men had known each other for years, yet it had always been an unequal partnership. In railway parlance, McEvoy was the engineer whilst Parker was the oily rag. There were nicer ways of putting it, but anyone observing the men for long would have recognized the metaphor. And yet none of that altered the fact that both men trusted each other with their lives, a situation that had been put to the test on many occasions in the past.

Thad took a quick glance around the sparsely occupied open carriage and decided that the time was probably right. They would reach Council Bluffs before long and he was not at all sure what they would come up against.

'Someone seems to be fighting the war all over again,' he stated flatly. He didn't have to look at Jud to know that he had his full attention. 'Two senators and one state governor slain within a month. All from Northern states and all of the expressed opinion that the South needs to bleed some more.'

His companion was quick to suggest the obvious motive for such crimes. 'What about simple robbery? I haven't met a politico yet who didn't have money.'

Thad offered him a wry smile that spoke volumes. 'The most recent attack involved our assassin somehow managing to persuade Governor Byron Taylforth to gallop headlong into the Missouri River and *then* he shot him in the back just to make certain. His body washed up on the far bank. If the local law is to be believed, he had one privately minted California gold piece in his pocket and a solid-silver fob watch. Of course, that might mean he actually had a whole lot more on his person before the marshal finished with him, but it still proves the point. Hell, even the dead bodyguard had cash money on him!'

Jud kept quiet. He sensed that there was more to come.

'Then again,' the other man continued, 'as an isolated incident, it *could* have involved revenge, or even a rival in love, but not with all three of them. And then there's the situation with the President.'

Jud felt his heartbeat increase. Ulysses Simpson Grant was a Northern war hero and therefore hated by many in the South. But what could these possibly related killings have to do with him?

'The railways have changed everything,' Thad remarked obliquely, as though that single fact suddenly explained all. 'There's nothing else like them in the world. California is now just six days' travel away from Washington. If Grant wants to get himself re-elected, he needs to reach out to *all* the voters in this vast country. Since he is not likely to attract many in the South, it makes a lot of sense for him to head west. At least that's what Attorney-General Williams told me before he sent us out here. Because it turns out that the President's going to be riding these very rails and passing through the very place where his governor was murdered. Kind of gives you pause, doesn't it?'

Jud appeared to be mesmerized. A solid, reliable young man from Pennsylvanian farming stock, he was not always too quick on the uptake, but this time there was no mistaking the potential danger.

'And I hear tell that even now Grant has only the one bodyguard,' he replied softly. 'When he can be bothered to use him, that is. Everybody says he doesn't like fuss.'

Thad nodded glumly. 'There's more to it than that. It seems that nobody learnt anything from Lincoln's death. He died in part because the one and only city constable ordered to watch his box at the theatre had drifted across the street to drink in a bar! Grant often travels around Washington without any kind of escort and nobody in government sees fit to comment on it.'

'What about the army?' his companion asked. 'Surely he'll be guarded on such a journey?'

'Oh yeah, General Sherman will detail some infantry for the train, but they'll just be there in case of Indian attacks and the like. They wouldn't expect an assault by white men.'

Jud was suddenly wide-eyed. 'So Mr Williams really thinks that there's a full-scale plot against the President?'

As though punctuating that question, the engine emitted a shrill whistle by way of announcing their arrival at Council Bluffs.

'That's what we're here to find out.'

Jared Barclay grimaced with pain as he eased his big frame into the swivel-chair. A small piece of shell fragment had ripped into his left buttock at Gettysburg and then had defied all the clumsy efforts of the battlefield surgeon to remove it. After enduring long moments of searing agony, Barclay had finally prodded the man with his bayonet and told him to desist. Since that time, there hadn't been a day that passed without the iron shrapnel reminding him of his presence at that bloodbath. The constant discomfort encouraged his feeling that the country somehow owed him a living, in any way that he chose to take it.

The discharged soldier's arrival at Council Bluffs had been mostly a matter of chance, influenced by the fact of its being on both a major steamboat and railroad route. Conveniently, his war service had easily enabled him to obtain employment as a lawman. As the duly appointed town marshal and completely lacking in any morals, Barclay had soon discovered more ways to make money than he could ever have imagined. So long as he locked up the drunks and broke up the occasional brawl, the city fathers left him to it. He was soon taking a percentage from nearly every commercial operation in Council Bluffs, as well as turning a blind eye to various dishonest activities. Yet one particularly ill-conceived chicken was about to come home to roost.

The jailhouse door opened and two young men strode in as though they owned the place. The marshal scrutinized them with practised eyes and didn't like what he saw. Where were his damned deputies when he needed them?

'If you're hunting celestials, you're in the wrong place,' he remarked coldly.

Thad fully understood the sarcastic reference to the Chinese tracklayers once employed by the Central Pacific Railroad and therefore his response was equally frosty.

'We don't work for any railroad, Marshal Barclay, and we're certainly not on the wrong side of the continent. *In fact*, I think we are exactly where we need to be.'

A dark frown appeared on the marshal's features. The

newcomers knew his name. There could be any number of reasons for that, but none of them boded well.

'You fellows have got the advantage of me,' he observed. 'I don't like that. And those are some pretty fancy irons you're packing there. If you're figuring on sticking around, you'd best hand them over before we talk some more. I run a peaceful town here.'

The two men made no move to hand over anything. Thad fixed his steely gaze on the beefy lawman. 'Why aren't you out chasing Governor Taylforth's murderer?' he snarled. 'That's what you do, isn't it? When someone gets shot dead within your jurisdiction? Form a posse?'

Ignoring the sudden spasm in his buttock, Jared Barclay leapt to his feet. The swivel-chair toppled noisily over as he placed a large, meaty hand on the butt of his revolver.

'Just who the hell are you sons of bitches?'

Thad favoured the marshal with a bleak smile, before slowly moving his hand towards an inner pocket of his jacket. 'I'm going to reach in for a wallet, so there's no cause to draw that *pistola*, savvy?'

Without ever taking his eyes from the lawman, he carefully extracted a thick leather holder. Opening it, he drew out an oilskin packet and then folded the wallet back on itself. With an almost dismissive gesture, he tossed it on to Barclay's desk. By divine coincidence a shaft of sunlight just happened to catch the highly polished brass shield and so highlighted the bold lettering surrounding the screaming eagle. US DEPARTMENT OF JUSTICE.

The town marshal's eyes almost popped out of their sockets as he took in the badge of office. His face was suddenly coated in a sheen of sweat that bore no relation to the temperature in the jailhouse. Apparently his two visitors worked for the newest and most senior law-enforcement agency in the country. They were directly answerable to the attorney-general and from what he had heard they could do pretty much what they damn well chose.

'Empty your pockets.' Thad's peremptory demand seemed to leave no room for discussion and caused Barclay's heart to miss a beat. Nevertheless, he didn't intend to buckle without a fight.

'The hell I will,' he replied heatedly. 'This is my town. What gives you the right to barge into *my* office and tell me what to do?' That question was barely out of his mouth before he regretted it.

Thad sighed impatiently. Opening the oilskin, he took out a folded sheet of paper.

'This document is signed by the Attorney-General of the United States of America and authorizes the owner of it to use any means necessary to uphold the law. In other words, I can demand assistance from the army and navy, requisition any train and utilize any telegraph network. I can also call on any lawman for help and remove him from office if I think fit. So I'll tell you again. Empty your pockets.'

Jared Barclay seemed to deflate before their eyes. Yet the visible aggression had now been replaced by something that they couldn't see. A meanness of spirit had always existed within him, but now a bitter vindictiveness was building up inside him. Any unpleasantness that occurred was only going to add to that and he certainly couldn't have imagined how bad things might get. With great reluctance he began to tip the contents of his pockets on to the desk. A kerchief, various keys and some small coins arrived first. Then came the objects that Thad had really been waiting for. Three privately minted Californian gold pieces dropped heavily from Barclay's clutches.

'Well, well,' muttered the federal officer as he scooped up the elaborate coinage. 'Seems like you've been indulging in a little private enterprise. We'll pass these on to the grieving widow.'

Without warning, his left hand abruptly streaked across the desk and grabbed the marshal's badge. Yanking hard, he took possession of both that and a sizeable chunk of linen.

'You should have stolen everything or nothing,' he snarled. 'Leaving a little something on the governor's body only made it easier for us and in turn made you an accessory to murder.'

At that moment the jailhouse door burst open and two young men displaying identical badges to that of their boss arrived. They were young and aggressive and their sharp eyes took in the damage to Barclay's shirt. Without even enquiring as to the reason, one of the deputies reached for his sidearm. Assuming that he was merely dealing with a troublesome trail hand, he grabbed it by the barrel to use as a club. It was that that saved his life. Jud levelled his Winchester and rammed its muzzle into the man's belly with tremendous force. With a howl of agony the unfortunate lawman doubled over and dropped to his knees on the floor. Before his startled companion could clear leather, he found himself staring into the gaping muzzle of Thad's Colt Army.

'Tell them who we are, *Marshal*,' he commanded. 'And

remember, you're in enough trouble already!'

'Rein in, boys. Turns out these two *gentlemen* are federal officers.' There was a note of weary resignation in Barclay's voice. His whole world had just turned upside down. As the threat of further violence receded he asked, 'So what happens now? I certainly didn't kill Taylforth and you can't prove that I did.'

Thad gazed at him contemptuously. 'We're really not interested in petty theft. We just want the name of the assassin. The man that you gave the run of this town to.'

The marshal was horrified. 'If I tell you that, I'm a dead man for sure!'

The federal enforcer favoured him with a bleak smile. He had not yet holstered his Colt and so merely pointed it at Barclay's left arm. Horrified disbelief suddenly registered on that individual's features. With a frightening crash the weapon discharged. A cloud of dense, sulphurous smoke filled the room, but there was no avoiding the agonized screams emanating from behind the desk.

'You crazy bastard,' hollered one of the deputies accusingly, although it was noticeable that he made no move to help his boss.

'Sweet Jesus, you've shot me,' the marshal finally managed. His arm was hanging at an abnormal angle and blood was soaking into the linen shirt. As his face turned deathly pale, he slumped back into the swivel-chair. Thad cocked his revolver and swept its aim around the desk. His face remained completely impassive as he placed the muzzle against Barclay's forehead.

'*The name!*'

CHAPTER THREE

Brett Dalton briefly eyed the nervous-looking saddle tramp standing before him and then allowed his gaze to switch back to the crumpled letter in his hand. It had travelled a long way and had been carefully packaged and sealed with wax to guard against tampering, but of course you could never be totally sure. The intelligence that it contained was of such importance that this time there had been no choice other than to entrust it to a courier. After all, the imminent movements of the President of the United States could hardly be relayed over the telegraph.

'How on earth does he find out this stuff?' he mused. Yet perversely it was the final sentence that entertained him the most.

It would very possibly be to everyone's advantage if the courier met with an accident, especially as it would save you having to pay him anything.

Dalton chuckled quietly as his cold eyes left the letter and settled on those of the foul-smelling messenger. Such action did nothing to reassure that twitchy individual. All the man wanted was to collect his money and be on his way. The black-garbed recipient of his sealed letter was an evil-looking son of a bitch who most definitely scared the bejesus out of him.

'You've done well finding me here,' that personage remarked softly. 'I'll wager you'll want to cut through the phlegm with some joy juice. Let's get you paid off and then you can get on down to that saloon. Who knows, there might even be some Dutch gal prepared to take you on.'

The prospect of ready cash and female company always allays fears and so it proved in this case. The man held out his hand expectantly as Dalton searched in his pocket for some coins. One neatly escaped his grasp and dropped to the floor. Greedily, the travel-stained envoy bent down to retrieve it, unaware that Dalton had silently slipped around behind him. As the luckless victim straightened up, a razor-sharp blade viciously sliced across his jugular. Warm, sticky blood sprayed out across the hotel bedroom. An anguished cry abruptly ceased and the fresh corpse collapsed heavily on to the carpet.

Dalton nodded his head in satisfaction before moving swiftly over to a basin. Fastidiously, he cleaned all traces of blood from the blade, dried it and then returned it to the sheath in his right boot. His stay in North Platte, Nebraska would now, of necessity, have to be curtailed. Bizarrely, it suddenly occurred to him that he seemed to leave a trail of dead bodies in his wake, but then that was the life that he had chosen. If the information in the letter was correct it was time to head further west to recruit some more guns. The job ahead was going to be the biggest that he had undertaken, and certainly the most profitable.

*

Sarah Barklam sniffed the air appreciatively. It was shaping up to be an unseasonably lovely day, offering as it did a brief but welcome respite from the normally stifling summer heat. A cooling wind had miraculously risen up and no amount of chores could detract from the joy that she felt. Simple pleasures come easily to the young and healthy.

Having hung the washing from the line at the side of the cabin, she drifted over towards the railroad track. Her dark, lustrous hair shone in the sunlight as she gazed at the iron rails stretching off into the distance. She had once been told that throughout most of the country they were exactly four feet, eight and one half inches apart and that fact strangely fascinated her. Although now a beautiful woman in her early twenties, she had never been interested in 'play pretties'. Always more of a 'tomboy', Sarah had been thrilled when her father had announced that he was taking on the water-pumping station for the rapidly expanding Union Pacific Railroad. The only drawback was its isolation. It was powerful hard to find any kind of a husband when living out in the wilderness near Lodgepole Creek on the Wyoming/Nebraska border.

She knelt down on the hardwood tie and placed her right ear to the nearest rail. The sound was as much felt as heard. A slight vibration that seemed to make her flesh tingle. The hum of the approaching 9.30 from Julesburg to Cheyenne. Getting lightly to her feet, she turned to view the huge, elevated water tank that had been constructed next to the tracks. That and the windmill used to pump up the water seemed to dwarf their home, but then of course that was the sole reason for their residing in such a lonely spot. The tiny settlement was the equivalent of a stage-coach way station. Just like humans, no steam locomotive could run without water and plenty of it.

Sarah gently sighed. Daydreaming wouldn't put food on the table and since the death of her mother all such tasks had fallen to her. The long gingham dress swayed around her slim legs as she walked briskly back to the wooden cabin. She was well aware that they were actually privileged to possess a timber building. Most private dwellings out on the plains were constructed from 'prairie marble' as sod was referred to. This primitive building block contained insects that could suddenly drop from the ceiling without any warning. Another disadvantage became unpleasantly apparent when the earth dried out in the baking summer heat. Clouds of dust and grit would again be deposited on the unhappy occupants. Fortunately for the Barklams, their home had been fash-ioned from some of the vast amount of wood brought out by train to create a railroad through the wilderness.

Tatum Barklam glanced up at her return and smiled infectiously. His lovely daughter never ceased to delight him, all the more so since she reminded him of his dear departed wife.

'Best get the coffee to boiling, gal. The Cheyenne train will be here soon and a good strong cup will set me up nicely.'

She returned his smile and began to stoke up the fire. The fact that he relentlessly made the same remark every morning did not bother her in the slightest. She gained comfort from the fact of always knowing when the next train was due. Security could be gained from routine.

What she couldn't hope to know was that not *all* trains kept to the timetable. Even the Union Pacific had to bend the knee occasionally!

The Department of Justice's special investigators were utilizing modern technology in a way that couldn't have been imagined only a few years earlier. Having left Council Bluffs and the Rock Island Railroad behind in the state of Iowa, they crossed the Missouri River and immediately found themselves in Omaha, Nebraska. Here they visited the office of the Pacific Telegraph Company. From there they contacted local lawmen in all the towns along the railroad in that state. Unsurprisingly the telegraph line ran parallel with the tracks across the entire width of the country.

Thad was searching for news of any shootists known to the law and of anything unusual that might have recently taken place in any of the main railroad towns in the state of Nebraska. Over the course of the afternoon he received negative replies from the settlements of Columbus, Grand Island, Cozad, Julesburg (strictly speaking in the Territory of Colorado) and Sidney. It was the eventual reply from North Platte that had the two men running for the Union Pacific Railroad depot.

'Why would a down-at-heel drifter have his throat cut in an upstairs room of the best hotel in town?' Thad was apparently putting the question to his companion, but really it was rhetorical, because he had already guessed the answer. 'Whoever could afford that room wanted him silenced because of something he knew and there's no surer way to achieve that than using a cutting tool on his jugular.'

As the two men steamed westwards towards the settlement of North Platte, Thad was painfully conscious of the fact that to his certain knowledge there was by then a very important special train wending its way out of New Jersey Avenue Station in Washington DC.

The short, stubby individual settled himself in a well-upholstered chair and drew deeply on his cigar. His full beard was turning grey and there was an air of melancholy about him that one would not have associated with a President of the United States seeking re-election. For in truth, Ulysses Simpson Grant did not really enjoy the responsibilities of his job. The formidable 'lion of war' had turned out to be a rather lamblike chief executive who was easily manipulated, but he had expensive tastes and quite simply needed the money.

As his Baltimore and Ohio Railroad carriage rolled on to the Thomas Viaduct, Grant's tired eyes were drawn to the sight of the world's first curved masonry railroad bridge stretching over the Patapsco River. The former commanding general reflected that his nation was actually capable of some amazing industrial feats that didn't involve the shedding of blood. The bend in the track also allowed him to view his special train without having to get up, and he was able to see the blue-clad figures of his soldiers seated at intervals on the roofs of the carriages. They were all equipped with Model 1866 'Trapdoor' Springfield breech-loading rifles of the type used along the Bozeman Trail in 1867.

No doubt the men were pleased about the change in routine, yet the fifty-year-old President couldn't help but view such exhibits with dismay. He hated all fuss and displays of pomp and had even managed to leave his personal body-guard behind in Washington, citing the fact that he had a 'whole damned trainload' of Sherman's men to watch over him. As a former soldier, he actually relished the thought of temporarily heading into the sparsely populated West and away from the politicians and favour-seekers infesting the nation's capital.

Who was to say that there might not even be a bit of excitement awaiting him out on the vast plains? And until that time, he did at least have a fresh bottle of Old Foresters finest bourbon to investigate. For the first time, such spirits were being sold in rather civilized sealed bottles as opposed to the old-fashioned kegs, and the distillers had very kindly presented him with a case to sample on his journey. Being president did have its benefits, so long as nobody tried to take the ultimate sanction against him as had happened to Lincoln only seven years earlier.

'That carpet came all the way from New York,' whined the hotelier. 'It's only been down for a month. Why the hell couldn't he have got himself murdered some place else?'

'You're all heart, Cy,' muttered North Platte's marshal as he firmly ushered the owner out of the room. As the door closed, he stated, 'Thought it best to leave the body here, once I got your telegram. Be glad to move him, though. Atmosphere's getting a bit unpleasant with this heat.'

'You did right, Marshal,' replied Thad warmly. 'And it's nice to get some willing cooperation for a change.'

'Don't like this kind of thing in my town,' the lawman stated. 'Don't like it at all.' He was no stranger to casual aggression, but the cold-blooded use of knives always unsettled him. 'With that huge Union Pacific depot here, we're trying to act civilized.'

The Justice Department investigator scrutinized the corpse, his nose twitching from the stench caused by the early stages of decomposition brought on by the summer heat. It lay on the fancy carpet in a pool of congealed blood. The blade had cut deep, so ensuring a swift death. The threadbare greatcoat and homespun linen, along with thick heavy shoes, told their own story.

'No money in any of the pockets, but I don't reckon that robbery came into it,' offered the marshal. 'From the state of his duds, I figure he arrived like that.'

'Anybody get a look at the killer?' asked Thad hopefully.

'One of the faro dealers caught a glimpse of him. Lean, sharp-featured fellow in a black suit. Said he looked like a real mean cuss.'

'And did he supply a name when he took the room?'

'Yeah. Actually, he did,' responded the marshal. 'Signed the register as a "Mister Grant".'

The two government men exchanged startled glances. It appeared that their prey had a twisted sense of humour and, from the description reluctantly supplied by Marshal Barclay, they knew it was definitely him all right, and that they were closing in. Thad carefully observed the local lawman before putting his next question.

'If a man wanted to hire some back-up, men with no scruples and a taste for violence, where would he go in this part of the world?'

The marshal didn't even have to ponder that one. 'Julesburg! It's a real snake-pit. The law's bought and paid for there. It might be a Union Pacific town, but so long as their operation is not affected the railroad doesn't really give a damn what goes on.' He eyed the two federal officers shrewdly. 'If you sent the same telegraph there that I got, then someone will likely know that you're coming.'

That thought had already occurred to Thad, but he kept silent. From the look on the local lawman's face that man obviously had more to impart.

'Julesburg was burnt to the ground by redskins back in '65. Hundreds of the varmints scalped and murdered many of the townsfolk in revenge for what Chivington did at Sand Creek. Sioux, Cheyenne, even Arapaho turned up for that party. It was only after the railroad arrived in '67 that the town was rebuilt, but most of the good citizens had been scared off. So now what you've got is nice new buildings filled with some real bad people. I suppose if you got into big trouble you could always cut on over to Fort Sedgwick, but the army don't like getting involved in civilian business unless they're ordered. That's if there's even any soldier boys left there. You'll probably know this already, but with the arrival of the iron horse a lot of the forts are being shut down.'

Thad smiled and patted his pocket ominously. 'We might just have to pay them a visit and try our luck. With the bona fides that we carry, those bluecoats will have to do as they're told.' He glanced over at Jud. 'It's too late in the day to try our hand over in Julesburg. Let's see if we can find a couple of rooms without blood on the carpet. It's been a pleasure, Marshal.'

As it turned out, Brett Dalton found out about his two pursuers from a totally unexpected informant. Marshal Jared Barclay now had to contend with two sources of pain, except that the damage to his left arm had nothing to do with the anonymous ranks of the Army of Northern Virginia. He knew exactly who was to blame and he wanted retribution. He also knew where his avenger was likely to be, because all the hardcases in the territory ended up in Julesburg at some point and his informed guesswork proved to be spot on. All it took was one carefully worded telegraph message.

The black-clad gunfighter surveyed his new recruits with vague distaste. His chosen profession was similar to theirs, except that to Dalton's all-seeing eye they appeared to be seedy and down at heel. Their tied-down guns and cold stares meant nothing to him. Anyone could adopt such a demeanour. What he needed was that they should be able to take orders without question and kill on demand.

They in turn viewed their new employer with suspicion and not a little unease. Most of them had heard the name 'Brett Dalton' but none of them had seen him in action. Yet there was no denying that he was a dangerous-looking *hombre* and he obviously had money, so for the time being they would eat his dust. Or at least most of them would.

'I've got a little test for some of you,' their new leader remarked blandly. 'There are two lawmen dogging my trail. I reckon six of you should be enough to handle them. The rest of us will head west to suss out the best spot to hold up a train. When you've finished your work, come right along after us. Wherever we are, it'll be within sight of the tracks.'

He had deliberately omitted to tell his men that his pursuers were actually federal officers. Murdering such men could bring more attention than some of his band would wish for. The ten gunhands digested his words for some moments before at last one of their number spoke up. They were in a dimly lit storeroom at the rear of the Double Deuce saloon-cum-hotel and the rising temperature only added to the man's simmering belligerence. He was a stocky, unshaven individual with grubby clothes and a mean expression.

'There's trains passing through this territory all day, every day, Dalton. What's so special about the one you're after? And why's the law after you? Just what are you wanted for, apart from dime-store hold-ups?'

Dalton's jaw line tightened. His normally cold grey eyes became chips of ice. Slowly he eased across the room until he was face to face with his interrogator.

'What's your name?' he hissed softly.

The other man held his gaze, but the fresh beads of sweat on his brow were no longer entirely due to the heat. No pistol-fighter liked to be so close to a possible opponent. The smell of fear suddenly mingled with that of rough-cut timber.

'Price,' came the sullen reply. 'Hector Price.'

'Well, Hector Price. My name is *Mister* Dalton until I say otherwise. And to show you I'm serious, I want you to draw that six-gun.'

Price's eyes widened slightly as the chilling reality of what was expected of him struck home. As his opponent's murderous stare bored relentlessly into him, he felt his palms turn clammy. Somehow he just knew that the other man would be faster. His armpits were soaked with sweat and the sudden terrifying notion assailed him that he might just die that day and not from 'lead pills' alone. At such point-blank range the muzzle flash would likely set his grubby shirt afire.

'Draw,' bellowed Dalton. Spittle from his lips caught Price's left cheek and made the gun thug flinch. Dalton's right hand hovered over the butt of his belly gun, whilst his left suddenly streaked out for a stinging, open-handed slap. The unexpected blow caused involuntary tears to well up in Price's eyes. The supreme confidence that Brett Dalton always felt before a kill showed on his face and in his stance. Hector Price made no move towards his own weapon. He was broken and he knew it.

Without taking his eyes off his subdued opponent, Dalton snarled, 'You don't want to get crosswise with me. Not any of you! You all do what I say, when I say and don't ever back-talk me. Understood?'

Only then did he glance around at the assembled men. None of them met his eyes and all of them muttered their assent. *Mister* Dalton nodded with grim satisfaction. Humbling the sons of bitches would hopefully give them a taste for revenge when his persistent pursuers finally showed up.

CHAPTER FOUR

'I've got a real bad feeling about this place!'

Jud Parker and Thaddeus McEvoy had just dropped down from the Union Pacific carriage and were standing next to the tracks, observing the town of Julesburg. And for sure it was certainly no 'jewel'. Surveillance was part of their job and Jud's comment had accurately reflected the feelings of both men. There was an immediately apparent and yet indefinable air of menace about the frontier settlement. It had a forlorn look about it that indicated a lack of civic pride and purpose. The replacement buildings had been built in a rush, using unseasoned timber and it showed. The structures didn't look to be weatherproof. There appeared to be gaps between the timber planking, as though the seams had opened.

'Good job this delightful town isn't a ship,' remarked Thad drily. 'It would have sunk by now.'

As their train rattled away on its westward journey towards Cheyenne the two men picked up identical carpetbags and slowly walked over to the town marshal's office. A couple of loafers leaning against a hitching rail regarded them with more than idle curiosity.

' 'Morning, boys,' offered Jud in a convincingly genuine attempt at sociability. 'Seems like a real quiet town you've got here.'

The two men sniggered as though appreciating a crude joke, before one of them chose to respond. 'Things ain't always what they seem, mister.'

There was little to be gained by slapping around the citizenry, so the two lawmen chose to ignore them and continued on to the marshal's office. Rather than barge straight on in, Thad chose instead to knock sharply on the untreated timber. There was a short silence before a petulant voice bellowed out, 'Don't you go beating on that goddamned door!'

Thad winked at his companion as he heaved against the poorly fitting door. The hinges squealed in protest as it opened stiffly. The justice man glanced around disdainfully at the flyblown office before allowing his gaze to settle on the room's only occupant. The tarnished tin shield indicated that he carried the law in Julesburg, but in truth he was a pitiful specimen. In a part of the world where there were very few fat men, this one broke the mould. He filled his swivel-chair like a bloated pig and did not look at all happy to see them. The remnants of a half-eaten meal were strewn across his desk.

'This had better be important,' the marshal whined as grease oozed over his many chins. 'I'm a busy man.'

'I can see that, but you're about to get busier,' snarled Thad as he displayed his gleaming badge of office. 'Stop feeding your fat face and pay attention. I need to know about any strangers who have arrived here recently.'

'Well, there's you for a start,' remarked the lawman with an inane chuckle.

Thad glanced at his companion and nodded. Jud grabbed one end of the overloaded desk and heaved it on to its side. As the marshal's food and drink abruptly ended in a slop pile at his feet, Thad stepped forward and slapped him hard across his fleshy features. 'You'd better start making sense or I'll kick you so hard you'll be wearing your ass for a hat. Now, I'll ask you again. Who's new in town?'

There was a moment's shocked silence as the corpulent lawman regarded them both with sullen, beady eyes. His cheek was bright red where the stinging blow had landed. Belatedly deciding that his unwelcome visitors were deadly serious, he noisily cleared his throat and began talking.

'I take it you ain't just looking for widows and orphans and such? Well, see now, there was a real mean-looking *hombre* over in the Double Deuce saloon last night. Seemed powerful keen on one of the painted ladies in there. He was suited-up like some city slicker.'

'He still in there?' Thad demanded.

'How should I know?' came the irritable response. 'I'm not his keeper.'

The federal officers exchanged meaningful glances and he added hastily, 'Depends on how many greenbacks he had to spend and just how welcome she made him. You know what it's like.'

Thad stared at him long and hard before apparently making up his mind. Abruptly turning away, he strode to the door with Jud trailing him out.

'Obliged for your assistance, Marshal,' he remarked sarcastically. 'Enjoy the rest of your meal.' With that, the door slammed shut and the two men were gone.

Julesburg's only law officer gazed bleakly after them for

a long time, before gradually a malicious smile registered on his fleshy face. He sighed and then, without any apparent reluctance, reached down into the wreckage that had been his lunch and scooped up a large piece of pie.

'What do you reckon?' Jud queried.

'I think half of what he said wasn't true and the other half was a goddamned lie,' his companion replied.

'So what are we going to do?'

'Visit the saloon of course, but not like lambs to the slaughter. We'll split up here. Find a back way in and get yourself situated. I'll hang loose for a while to give you time. And remember, you just may well not be the only one hankering after a back room.'

With that the two men went their separate ways. As he tramped off through the powdery dust, it occurred to Jud that he might quite possibly have to kill someone that day, but then in his line of work it wouldn't be the first time.

'That bastard Dalton's going to pay for riding me like that!'

'You're all talk, Hec Price. Yeah, he put the shits up you good, but if you want paying for this job there's not a damn thing you can do about it. Save your bile for whoever comes looking.'

The two sweating gun thugs were hunkered down in a first-floor room, impatiently fingering their firearms. The door was wide open, allowing them a good view of the saloon below, but even so there was little airflow to provide relief from the heat.

'We don't even know who or what they are,' responded Price petulantly.

'Who cares?' snarled his companion. 'Six on one, six on two. However you cut it, it'll be no dog fall for them!'

Their four cronies were secreted in various parts of the building. They all knew their trade well enough to realize the value of height in any conflict, so two of them were in another room off the far landing. The remaining pair were waiting in the same dark, windowless storeroom at the rear of the Double Deuce where Dalton had held his highly charged meeting. There they were marginally cooler, but had to keep the door almost closed to avoid discovery.

The lank-haired, greasy proprietor was perspiring worst of all. His barkeeper was laid up with a distemper of the bowels, which meant that he very reluctantly had to fill in. He knew exactly what was afoot, but was under pain of death to stay right where he was and serve the regulars. Every footfall made him twitch and it was all he could do to remain upright. 'By Christ,' he fumed silently. 'What have I done to deserve this?'

Jud levered a cartridge into the firing-chamber of his Winchester and regarded the closed door speculatively. If it were he who had men staking out the saloon, then he would place at least one of them in a back room. And any attempt to barge straight on in would leave him highlighted by the midday light. Yet he didn't have time to pussyfoot around. Thad would soon be going in through the front entrance.

After taking a deep breath the Justice Department officer stood to one side and rapped firmly on the rough-cut timber. From inside there came a brief scuffling noise followed by silence. Oh, there was someone in that room all right. Again Jud's knuckles struck the door, only this time he followed it up.

'Open up, do you hear? I've got a wagonload of rotgut to unload and if I don't get these kegs inside, there'll be hell to pay.'

From beyond the threshold came muffled cursing followed by footsteps. A bolt was carefully eased back by someone clearly keen to make as little noise as possible. The door creaked open and the moment had come. Yet Jud was a lawman dealing with someone whose identity was unknown and whose hostility was unproven. Lethal force was quite unacceptable. So, as a set of bearded features came into view, he reversed his carbine and slammed the butt into the man's temple. With an awful moan that individual collapsed to the floor and in the process wedged the door open. Without hesitation, Jud leapt through the opening, scuttled round behind the door and dropped down on to his haunches. Part of the large room was still shrouded in gloom. If there was anyone else there, he couldn't see him and could only wait impatiently for his eyesight to adjust.

Thaddeus McEvoy swept rapidly through the swing doors. He edged off to his left, then backed up until his shoulders were pressed against the wall. His sharp eyes swiftly scrutinized the interior. A few dissolute drinkers lounged at the tables. Given the time of day, the resident whores were absent, very probably catching up on their sleep. To his practised gaze, certain things were immediately apparent. The barkeeper was scared out of what wits he possessed, and two upstairs rooms were either vacant and being aired or the occupants strangely chose to keep the doors wide open. Everything was suddenly very clear to him, as was his course of action.

With every appearance of outward calm Thad made his way over to the long, heavy bar. It ran almost the full length of the right-hand side of the room and looked to be proof against 44/40 cartridges and the like.

'What'll it be, mister?' The temporary barkeeper croaked out the question and appeared to be in an itching hurry to run for the nearest exit.

'Let's start with some information and then just maybe I'll move on to a drink,' replied Thad softly as he unhurriedly lowered his carpetbag to the floor.

'What do you reckon? Is it him?'

'How the hell do I know?' Price whispered back testily. 'We don't even know who *him* is. Just keep listening.'

The two men had their rifles levelled, but it was not an easy shot due to the presence of a wooden handrail running round the upper landing.

Then, in the storeroom, a weapon discharged with a thunderous roar and Jud suddenly knew for certain that his boss had been correct. There was a blast of air close by his right ear as the projectile slammed into and then out of the thin timber wall. His opponent's muzzle flash had been there for all to see and the time for prudence was past. Pulling the stock up to his cheek, Jud took rapid aim and returned fire.

The first gunshot set off a chain reaction that was unstoppable. The sweat-drenched barkeeper ceased all attempts at maintaining civility and simply dropped out of sight. Galvanized into action, Thad leapt up on to the counter and slid down behind the bar. As he did so a bullet slammed into the solid timber. The flurry of heavy footsteps that followed suggested that the saloon's entire clientele had fled. From the storeroom came more shooting, but it might as well have been on the moon. Jud would have to take care of himself for the time being.

'You reach for any kind of weapon and I'll kill you,' snarled Thad to the quivering barkeeper.

That individual regarded him through eyes like saucers. 'I believe you, mister. For Christ's sake, I only asked you what you were drinking.'

Completely ignoring him, the government man shuffled sideways a few paces. Swiftly rising up, he snapped off a shot at the landing. Within four walls the detonation was actually painful. From directly above him a voice bellowed out, 'Where the hell is he, Price? We've got no shot from here.'

'Behind the bar, dummy. Get over here and help us out!'

The prospect of the assassins joining forces gave Thad an idea. He levered in another cartridge and again shifted position as protection against return fire. Another voice boomed out from above.

'We're coming over. Give us some cover.'

A fusillade of shots came from the opposite landing and chunks of lead slammed into the bar. The barkeeper moaned with fear as wooden splinters showered over them, but Thad kept his head down and remained calm. His barricade was actually of a stronger construction than the building itself and he had no desire to hinder the movements of the men upstairs. He wanted them in one place.

The pounding of heavy boots on bare floorboards

ended at the same time as the shooting. Taking that as his cue, Thad leapt up and fired three rapid shots at the kerosene lamp fixed in a wall bracket next to the bedroom opposite. As the glass shattered, burning liquid showered over the wall and floor. On bone-dry timber the flames took hold almost immediately.

'That should give those bastards something to think about.' There was no disguising the satisfaction in his voice. As always in a fight, Thad found himself succumbing to a heady exhilaration.

'Oh, Christ!' responded the barkeeper mournfully. 'First it was the Cheyenne dog soldiers and now it's your turn. Where the hell's the law when you need it?'

A volley of shots came from the group on the landing. The flames affected their aim and all the projectiles went high, shattering the huge mirror behind the bar. At such close range the effect was both awesome and terrifying. Shards of glass tumbled over the two crouching men. Blood was dripping from his neck as the barkeeper yelled out in pain and anger.

'You poxy cockchafers. That mirror came all the way from New York.'

Up against so many guns, Thad could only stay put, but he was relatively unconcerned by the turn of events. The fire had taken hold on the upper storey. Nothing and no one was going to stop it and his assailants suddenly had far more to worry about than any number of lawmen.

'Sweet Jesus, we're all going to burn to death!'

The landing had become a raging inferno. Flames were licking up the bedroom walls. The very air felt as though it was burning. As Thad had surmised, the gunslingers no longer gave a damn about anyone down in the saloon, because their own survival was suddenly in doubt.

'Out through the windows,' yelled Hec Price. 'It's our only chance.' With that he began to smash the wooden frames out with the butt of his Henry rifle. More shards of glass fell, but this time into the street.

'What's occurring, Thad?' Jud's voice bellowed out from the storeroom. There was blood on his face, but he sounded in full fettle.

'Those sons of bitches are trapped. Their only way out is through the windows. Keep clear of here and scoot round to the front. I'll meet you there.' Turning to the barkeeper, the justice man added, 'This building's lost. If you value your worthless life, follow me!'

Without waiting for a response, he turned away and began crawling towards the main entrance. Scuffling noises behind him confirmed that the sorry-looking proprietor had taken his advice. The bar protected both men until the last few yards. Thad fired once at the blazing bedroom and then broke cover. As he expected, there were no answering shots. The men upstairs were far too preoccupied with smashing out the window.

Jud was poised at the front corner of the building. The moment that he saw his boss emerge, he aimed his Winchester at the first-floor room and fired blindly.

'Throw all your weapons out,' he yelled. 'Any of you murdering bushwhackers that climbs out toting firearms gets shot.'

As Jud's bullet slammed into the wall behind him Hec Price jumped back from the window. They were between a rock and a hard place and he knew it. Flames were consuming the bedroom and the heat was unbearable. All of them were choking from the smoke that billowed around.

God damn that Dalton for getting them into this mess.

'I'm coming out,' he hollered frantically, without even consulting his cronies. As his guns hit the dirt street, he sat on the windowsill and twisted around to grip it with both hands. A shard of glass sank deep into his left palm, causing him to cry out in agony. With his legs dangling loose, he simply let go and dropped to the hard ground.

So far so good, but it was then that everything turned sour. Unable to control his landing, Price hit the ground hard. An ankle turned under him, either broken or badly sprained and he sprawled out into the street. With stabbing pains in his leg and blood pouring from his left hand, he had lost the ability for rational thought. Instinctively, he reached out for his nearest discarded weapon.

'Don't be a fool,' yelled Thad, swinging his carbine around to cover the man.

It made no difference. Price's right hand closed around the smooth, comforting butt of his revolver and the lawman fired. The outlaw's torso jerked under the savage impact of the large-calibre bullet and he suddenly lay still.

'I told him not to reach for it,' Thad exclaimed angrily as he kicked the man's weapons away. As a peace officer he deeply regretted all unnecessary killing.

'It's a trap,' howled one of the men in the room above. 'They're just going to shoot us down like dogs!' With that, he poked his Spencer out of the window and opened fire. Out of sheer desperation his two companions did the same, but none of them were able to enjoy the benefits normally expected when shooting from cover. One half of their room was consumed by fire and their clothes were scorching on their backs. They could smell their own hair singeing. Under such circumstances taking steady aim was impossible.

With hot lead churning up the street around them, the two lawmen stood their ground and returned fire. Rapidly working the lever actions of their Winchesters, they sent a number of well-aimed shots up into the doomed building. First one man was hit and then another. Both took head wounds and fell back into the blazing inferno. The last gunfighter was claimed solely by the advancing flames and collapsed in writhing agony. His screams seemed to last interminably as finally the whole room was claimed by the fire.

As the two justice men backed off in the face of mounting heat they seemed to be followed remorselessly by the sickly sweet smell of burning flesh. The conflagration was spreading to take in the whole building, which was quite obviously doomed. Its owner, temporarily subdued by the brutal violence, could only stand and watch in glum silence.

With the end of one specific threat, Thad began to glance around at their surroundings. The whole town had turned out to watch the spectacle, albeit at a safe distance. There was little apparent concern over the blaze spreading, because the townsfolk had learned from the first disaster and the buildings were now well spaced. However, the gunfire had actually been sufficient to drag the marshal away from his feast. Once certain that the hostilities were over, that individual began plodding his way heavily towards the scene.

It was then that Thad felt a hand tightly grip his ankle. Twisting around in alarm, he looked down to find Price still clinging on to life. Blood was trickling out of his mouth and he obviously hadn't got long to go.

'That Dalton will settle for you, law dog,' he gasped weakly. 'Once he's taken the train.'

The hairs stood up on the back of Thad's neck. He glanced at Jud in alarm before putting the question. 'What train?'

The stricken gun thug managed a faint chuckle before falling back and lying still. He was quite dead. In stark contrast, the justice man's thoughts whirled like a maelstrom. All his suspicions appeared to be correct. The paid assassin really was after the President. Jud had had the sense to remain silent and was standing waiting on instructions.

'Did you leave anyone alive round the back?' Thad demanded. In response to an affirmative nod, he continued, 'Get him away from that fire and cuff him to something solid. He's got a lot of talking to do. *Don't* take him anywhere near that jailhouse.' Recalling that the barkeeper was near by, he added softly, 'I'm going to find the telegraph office. We need to try and stop Grant's train before it gets near this assassins' den!'

As Jud raced off around the side of the doomed building, Thad turned to face the florid marshal. Before either of them could say anything, the saloonkeeper launched into a torrent of complaint.

'Jesus H. Christ, Jared. Where the hell have you been? This madman's torched my place. Everything's gone. I want him locked up tighter than a gnat's ass until the circuit judge arrives, you hear? *A gnat's ass!*'

As if to punctuate that strident demand there came a sudden burst of explosions from deep inside the blazing ruin. Flames had obviously reached the box of cartridges in Thad's carpetbag. Instinctively backing away, the town marshal glanced nervously over at the justice man. Living on the frontier, he was no stranger to casual violence, but the level of death and devastation that had suddenly struck his town was unheard of since the Indian depredations. His possible knowledge of the ambush would likely remain unproven, but he knew that he should best make himself scarce. Placing a podgy hand on the saloon-keeper's shoulder, he firmly propelled him away from his disintegrating premises. As they moved off down the street, the marshal patiently explained Thad's official position.

'*A lawman!*' came the astounded cry. 'He's worse than the goddamned Sioux!'

CHAPTER FIVE

As it happened, it wasn't until later that afternoon that any telegraph messages reached the President's special train. Grant had swiftly discovered that by living on the move he had partially escaped from the relentless calls of office and he was enjoying it. It was only when they stopped at any sizeable habitation that communications from Washington caught up with him. Not that they all came from back East.

'You mean to tell me that I'm supposed to kick my heels in your town until further notice, all because you've received telegraphed word of a *possible* threat to me? Do you realize just how many times I came under fire in the recent conflict?'

President Ulysses Simpson Grant chewed heavily on his cigar as he stared wide-eyed at North Platte's marshal. That individual, whilst undoubtedly uncomfortable in the presence of a living legend, was nevertheless determined to do his duty as he saw it.

'From what I've seen of Thad McEvoy, he and his partner know their business. If he believes there to be a plot to take your life then you must take it seriously, sir.'

'*Must* doesn't come into it, Marshal,' Grant growled ominously. 'My God, man, have you seen how many soldiers Sherman has foisted on me? How can a few petty road agents stop this train? Answer me that.'

'There's more than one way to skin a cat, Mr President,' the lawman answered ambiguously.

Skin a cat, mouthed the soldier turned politician incredulously. 'And just who the hell is this McEvoy anyway? I've never even heard of him.'

The answer to that came from a dour, heavily bearded individual sitting comfortably in one of the railway carriage's luxuriously appointed armchairs. As the only member of Grant's cabinet accompanying him on the re-election campaign and with an eye firmly fixed on his own future, Secretary of the Interior Columbus Delano had ensured that no detail too small had escaped him.

'I'm told that he's the new Justice Department's most exceptional agent. Then again,' he added drily, 'if you believe Attorney-General Williams, all his agents are exceptional.'

Grant leaned back in his chair and drew deeply on his cigar. His eyes flitted between the two men as he weighed up the situation. George Williams was no fool. If he had men active along the route of the presidential train, it was because he saw a need for it. Then again he, Grant, was as stubborn and ornery as any mule. He had an election to win and no goddamned bandits were going to affect that. Mind made up, he announced his decision.

'We'll spend the rest of the day here in your fine town, Marshal. I'll give the good folks of North Platte a speech that they'll remember for the rest of their days. What say you to that, Columbus? They were well suited to it in

Cozad yesterday, were they not?'

Delano groaned inwardly, but managed to produce a smile of sorts. The President was a short, stubby individual with no great gift for oratory. The interest shown in him was due more to his undoubted fame as a general and the novelty of having the nation's chief executive visiting the frontier.

'I'm sure it will do them all a power of good, Mr President,' he responded smoothly.

Grant blew a great plume of smoke towards the ceiling and nodded slowly. He knew that he was being humoured and consequently his next words came out like chips of ice.

'Tonight we will enjoy whatever hospitality this town has to offer, but tomorrow morning we're on our way to Wyoming and the devil take any miserable outlaws that get in my way!'

The Cheyenne train had taken on water and was long gone. There was not even the slightest vibration on the tracks. Sarah Barklam had a rug hanging from a line and was vigorously beating the dust out of it. The sun's rays shone down on her relentlessly. Sweat formed upon her top lip and she eventually stopped to get her breath. It was shaping up to be a hellishly hot day. So much so that all she could think of was getting inside and slaking her thirst. Thanks to the Union Pacific's windmill and storage tank, water was one thing they were not short of.

It was as she chanced to gaze back down the tracks in the direction of Sydney, Nebraska, that she first saw them. Through the heat haze, she could just make out five individual dots moving towards her. The young woman's brow furrowed in a display of puzzlement. Due to the dominating presence of the railroad, visitors on horseback were a fairly rare occurrence and yet they weren't likely to be Indians. When any of the savage tribes chose to appear, they just seem to materialize without any prior warning. Which meant that the riders must be white and quite possibly poor, if they couldn't afford the price of a train ticket. At their rate of approach it would be some time before they reached her, so Sarah dragged the rug off the line and moved indoors. In all innocence, she decided that it would be nice to have some company around the place, even if it was likely to be just for a short time.

Brett Dalton sat astride his motionless horse and carefully scrutinized the isolated clutch of buildings. The burning heat was becoming almost intolerable, but he refused to rush, because that was when mistakes were made. He was conscious of his four companions waiting impatiently at his side, but he paid them no heed. They were cannon fodder on wages and would do as they were instructed. Finally he nodded his satisfaction. It would do perfectly. Even the telegraph line ran past the cabin, parallel to the tracks.

'Whoever we encounter over there, you leave all the talking to me, savvy?' He waited for each of the men to nod his agreement before continuing. 'Don't speak unless you're spoken to and even then stick to grunts and one-word answers. That way you won't mess up and nobody will have to die. Yet!'

Sarah peered out of the window and saw that they were nearly upon her. Since her father was at the Union Pacific depot in Cheyenne for part of the day, it was up to her to greet them. On the spur of the moment she pulled on a bonnet, so as to provide some shade from the punishing sunlight. The wide brim hid her delightful features, whilst the white material contrasted perfectly with her dark, flowing hair. Never having suffered any bad experiences at the hands of her own race, it never occurred to her to be wary of the newcomers. Consequently, her father's Henry rifle remained tucked away in the corner of the room. She pulled open the door and swept lithely out to greet the five men.

As the cabin door burst open, Dalton's right hand moved towards his belly gun. An obviously young woman was moving swiftly towards them, but a snow-white bonnet obscured her face. As she was apparently unarmed, he allowed his hand to fall away as he reined in. It was his intention to take control of the cabin and everyone in it. Should anyone resist, then so much the worse for them. But, with all carefully laid plans, there are often variables that cannot be foreseen.

Sarah lifted her head high, so as to view the travellers. With a soft, 'Hello gentlemen,' she beamed a delicious smile of welcome, which only faltered slightly when she got her first good look at the horsemen. It was then that the initial feelings of unease entered her thoughts. Dalton, on the contrary, was temporarily and quite unexpectedly lost for words. Unlike the young lady, who had five people to view, all his concentration was focused on her. *Sweet Jesus, but she's beautiful,* he decided, his mind in a whirl.

His companions were of a similar opinion, but where he was struck by her sheer exquisiteness, they were concerned only with raw lust. For long moments, whilst their leader was incapacitated, they regarded her in brooding silence, licking their lips and mentally undressing her. Taking control of the pumping station suddenly seemed to be an exceptionally good idea.

Recognizing the smouldering scrutiny for what it was, Sarah was swiftly assailed by real fear and took an involuntary step backward. It was then that Brett Dalton found his voice. Conscious of the thoroughly unsavoury appearance of his crew, he favoured the delectable young woman with an uncommonly genuine smile as he introduced himself.

'Sincere apologies if we have startled you, miss. Only we are a mite windblown from travelling and not at our best.'

With an effort, Sarah concentrated her attention on the speaker rather than his dubious-looking cronies. She had to admit that he appeared to be considerably more prosperous and a great deal more attractive than the others.

Gathering herself, she replied, 'There is a hand pump around the side of our cabin. You and your . . . friends are welcome to the water, Mister—'

He had not missed her use of the word *our*. 'Brett. The name's Brett.' He did not elaborate as to whether that was a Christian name or surname, but instead continued with, 'That's real kindly of you. We are on our way to Cheyenne, but this heat is beyond tolerating. We figured to maybe camp here for a while, if that would set right with your husband.'

Completely ignoring the others, Sarah regarded him carefully. He possessed a hard, uncompromising appearance that she found strangely attractive and she knew that she too had made an impression on him. Intuitively, she decided that he meant her no harm and so she replied with complete honesty.

'I am unmarried, Mr Brett. I live here with my pa. He holds this place for the Union Pacific. Right now he is in Cheyenne, but will be back before nightfall. Unlike you, he prefers to avail himself of the railroad service.'

Dalton's eyes remained glued to hers as he responded. He was loath to end the conversation, as he knew that it would break the contact.

'Sadly, we have temporarily fallen on hard times, but we have a job of work to complete that should return us to prosperity, Miss—?' So saying, he dismounted and stepped forward in one fluid movement.

Appearing momentarily flustered, she nevertheless responded with, 'Sarah. Sarah Barklam.'

He smiled and proffered his hand, which after a brief hesitation she accepted.

'A pleasure, Miss Sarah. I certainly never expected to come across someone such as yourself out here.'

A feminine touch was not new to him, but mostly they came from so-call 'soiled doves' rather than an obviously chaste young lady. Her fingers were long and slender and he had a sudden urge to kiss the back of her hand, which was only resisted with difficulty. The two of them remained linked for far longer than was strictly appropriate, until at last he blurted out, 'Yes, well then, I guess we'd better leave you to your chores.'

With that, he tore himself away and turned to his men. With a curt gesture, he indicated that they should follow him. Reluctantly they tore their licentious glances from the young woman and tagged along. Sarah watched them head for the pump. No longer under scrutiny herself, she was at last able to think rationally, and with that ability came some serious qualms. If the man named Brett had indeed fallen on hard times, then why did he appear so prosperous? Although covered in trail dust, his suit appeared to be of excellent quality and, unlike the others, he had healthy-looking skin and apparently good teeth. And why would someone like him even associate with four saddle tramps? The more that she thought about it, the less it made sense. One thing was for sure. She would be very glad when her father returned.

Brett Dalton would not have admitted the fact to anyone, but for the first time in many years he was flustered. The Barklam woman had completely taken his breath away. He could never have expected to encounter someone as fragrant as her in such an out-of-the-way shit hole. Yet he had, and such a situation was dangerous. Already she had caused him to alter his plans. By suddenly not wishing to show his dark intentions, he had left her in control of the cabin. In itself that fact mattered little, but he couldn't allow personal feelings to jeopardize his plans.

Dragging himself out of his reverie, Dalton addressed his men. They had all slaked their thirst at the hand pump and were now allowing the horses to drink from a trough.

'I'll be gone for a while. Keep out of the cabin and stay away from the woman. Anyone lays a finger on her, I'll cut it off! Savvy?'

The four men recognized the latent menace in his voice and all nodded reluctantly. One of them, by name of Brad Taylor, did have the wit to ask a sensible question.

'What if her pa comes back? What do we do with him?'

'You do nothing to nobody,' their leader replied. 'Let Miss Barklam do the talking and keep your heads down.'

With that, Dalton mounted up and rode off without a backward glance. He allowed his horse to pick his way over the railway tracks and then headed off towards the hills beyond. His departure had not gone unnoticed. Sarah watched him through the ancient bull's-eye glass in the cabin's single window as he moved off. It seemed very strange behaviour if, as he had said, the heat was *beyond tolerating*. Why hadn't he told her he was leaving? And where on earth could he be going? There wasn't another dwelling for miles around. A pit of anxiety formed in her stomach as she realized that his four companions remained outside. She had seen how they had looked at her and now they no longer had Mr Brett to keep them in check.

After a moment's consideration, she moved over to where her father's rifle leaned against the wall. Taking it firmly in hand, the young woman worked the lever slowly. She had fired the weapon many times at targets and was not daunted by its power, the way many females might be. With a cartridge in the firing chamber, she went over to the sturdy wooden table and sat down. Sarah pointed the Henry directly at the door and felt her natural confidence return. If any of those men attempted anything unpleasant they would get much less than they wanted and far more than they could handle.

Tatum Barklam stared out of the window with unseeing eyes. Normally when he rode the rails back from Cheyenne he liked to stand up front in the cab and pass the time with the crew. There he could absorb the noise and smells of the steam engine as it unleashed its awesome energy. Yet on this trip the landscape passed by unnoticed.

The news that he had received at the Union Pacific depot had been both exciting and shocking. Unbelievably, President Grant himself was heading west on a special train, which both logically and yet quite amazingly would need to take on water at the Barklam's pumping station. As a former Northern supporter of the Union, such an event would be cause for celebration, were it not for the additional information that now consumed Tatum's every thought.

Apparently there was the very real possibility of a plot against the President's life. Since the army couldn't hope to cover all the miles of track, the railroad was warning its employees to be on their guard. News of any strangers should be reported by telegraph immediately. And there was the rub. His cabin wasn't equipped to receive messages without someone climbing up a pole and connecting a telegraph key to the wire. In all innocence he had left his daughter alone when a band of hired killers could be on the loose. He had already lost his wife to disease. The notion of anything happening to Sarah just didn't bear thinking about.

'For Christ's sake,' he mused despairingly, 'can't this train move any faster?'

CHAPTER SIX

As afternoon advanced into evening, the enervating heat began to ebb and the men started to grow restive. They had passed the time languishing in the shade of the massive elevated water tank. For a short while they had contemplated releasing a stream of water over themselves, but none of them could be bothered to discover how it worked. In any case, they had long ago become accustomed to the stink of their unwashed bodies. Dalton's continued absence puzzled them and also paved the way for a darker turn of events.

'Where the hell can the son of a bitch have got to?' whined one of them called Nelson.

'There's nothing else out here worth a damn.'

'He's probably sitting up on one of those hilltops waiting to see what we do,' remarked Brad Taylor, who seemed to possess the most intelligence of the four.

'The hell with *Mister* Dalton,' snarled a man named Forrest. 'What are we going to do with that little lady over in the cabin?'

'Doesn't seem right that she's sitting in there all on her lonesome,' added the fourth gun thug, who went by a number of aliases, but who had recently settled on Van Dorn, simply because he liked the highborn sound of it. 'What say we pay her a visit? There'd be no harm in it and who knows, she might even get to like us.'

One of them chuckled suggestively and then all four of the stinking, sweat-stained trouble-causers clambered to their feet. If they had had more than just the delightful Sarah Barklam on their minds, they might have noticed that the iron rails had started to vibrate very slightly.

Over in the cabin, that young lady heard the approaching footsteps and her blood turned cold. All afternoon she had been wondering when they would get around to her and now the time had come. Knowing that she couldn't cover them all from the doorway, Sarah retreated to the corner of the room. Cocking her rifle, she prayed for the mysterious Mr Brett to return. Somehow she had sensed that he at least did not mean her any mischief.

By coincidence, she suddenly heard two noises at once. There was a loud knocking on the cabin door and the more distant sound of an approaching train. Which meant that her father would soon be home and, being unarmed, might quite possibly be in mortal danger himself.

'Open up, missy,' called out Van Dorn playfully. 'We don't mean you any harm. We just want some vittles, that's all.'

'All of you will stay outside,' she boldly shouted back. 'I have a repeating rifle and I know how to use it.'

The door suddenly flew open with tremendous force, causing Sarah to jump with surprise. The four men were grouped around the threshold and she began to tremble slightly.

'There's no cause to be unfriendly,' remarked Forrest.

He hawked a stream of chewing tobacco into the dirt before advancing into the cabin. As his three companions swaggered in after him, Sarah drew in a deep breath to calm her nerves and gestured threateningly with the rifle.

'Don't any of you come closer or I'll fire,' she stated firmly.

Brad Taylor regarded her speculatively. 'Have you ever killed anyone, girl? Because there's a whole world of difference between taking someone's life and just shooting at rocks and such.'

Sarah stared at him in horror and just couldn't find any words with which to answer. The four men had spread out into a semicircle around her and were gazing at her intently. Lust was mingling with the sort of excitement that they normally felt before a kill. They rarely entered into any gunplay unless the odds were firmly on their side. So intent were they on the young woman that the arrival of the train completely failed to register with them.

Tatum viewed the four grazing horses with horrified alarm. Where were their riders and, more to the point, where was his daughter? He leapt to his feet, ran for the carriage's open platform and waited impatiently for the train to lose speed. It was then that he heard the muffled gunshot. Almost beside himself with worry, Tatum dropped down from the moving carriage. The engine had nearly come to a halt next to the water tank and he managed to keep his balance. He was a fit, active man in his late forties and had no problem sprinting for the cabin. All his attention was focused on that, so he was totally oblivious to the surprised looks of the engine's crew. Such was the noise in the cab that they had not heard the shot.

With his heart thumping like an anvil, Tatum reached the entrance and peered in. The scene was chaotic and did nothing to soothe his fears. A pall of sulphurous smoke hung in the room. One man, a complete stranger, was on his knees crying out with pain and anger. He was clutching his right shoulder, which was covered in blood. Sarah was lying on the floor groaning. The Henry rifle lay next to her.

'The bitch really did it,' wailed the wounded man. 'For Christ's sake, look at me. I'm shot!'

In actual fact, no one was looking at the self-styled Van Dorn. Considering their relative lack of intelligence, his three companions reacted with great speed to Tatum's sudden arrival. One of them, Forrest, reached down and grabbed Sarah by the hair. Yanking her painfully to her feet, he placed a cocked revolver to her head and commanded, 'Don't you move, railroad man, or she takes a lead pill!'

The other two drew their weapons and pointed them at her father. Brad Taylor gazed through the window at the stationary train waiting expectantly next to the water tank. Remarkably, he immediately knew what needed to be accomplished. 'Get out there, mister. Do what's necessary and send them on their way with a big smile. Any little thing that doesn't look right to us and the girl takes a ball in the head. I'm guessing that you wouldn't like that over much.'

Tatum stared at his daughter in horror. Blood was trickling from her nose and she was obviously dazed, but otherwise she appeared to be unharmed. He had to keep her that way. From the engine cab there came a shouted enquiry from the fireman.

'Hey, Tatum. Are you all right in there?'

Nelson, a thin-featured consumptive, rasped out his own harsh instructions.

'Answer him, *Tatum*. Make things right out there and then wander back in here, like you haven't got a care in the world. Savvy?'

The railroad employee struggled to take in the sudden turn of events. His mind was a whirling maelstrom of conflicting emotions. What stirred him into action was the sure knowledge that Sarah's survival depended on what he did next. Backing carefully out of their cabin, he offered a wave of acknowledgement to the fireman and then began an unhurried walk over to the water tank. Once there, he took hold of a thick rope and pulled hard on it. A long metal funnel that had been nestling vertically against the caulked wooden tank swung down, so that its mouth hung directly over the engine's own tank.

'Christ almighty, Tatum,' offered the engineer, who had dropped down out of the cab to stretch his legs. 'You look like you've seen a ghost. What ails you, man?'

Tatum pulled another cord to release the water before favouring the other man with a weak smile. 'That damned beef that they gave me back in Cheyenne must have been tainted. My guts are churning something powerful.'

At least part of that statement was the truth and it seem to satisfy the engineer, who replied sagely, 'Ha, there's no such thing as a free lunch. They always come back to haunt you. Set yourself down in the privy for a spell and you'll be right as rain.'

With that he turned and wandered back to his cab. In reality he was keen to be off. The heat was still unpleasant and at least there was a breeze when they were on the move. In no time at all the engine's tank was full and Tatum heaved on another rope to shut off the stream of water. As the funnel returned to its resting place, the fireman waved his thanks and closed the cover on the locomotive. If Sarah's father was ever going to summon help it had to be now. And yet it was that intimate relationship that stopped him. Not even the possibility of a threat to the President's life could count for much against that of his daughter's. She was all that he had left.

With bitter resignation, he turned away from the train and all its passengers and headed back towards captivity or worse. As he trudged along, Tatum noticed the intruders' discarded saddles. A scabbard attached to each one held either a rifle or carbine, but they might as well have been in California for all the good that they were to him. The only weapon that really counted was the revolver held to Sarah's head.

As the train slowly pulled away, the engineer hollered after him.

'Remember, treat yourself to a good shit, Tatum. Ha, ha, ha.'

Brett Dalton lay at the peak of the reverse slope, a small pair of field glasses held to his eyes. He watched with interest as a man leapt from the moving carriage and rushed for the cabin. Since there was no sign of his own motley crew, it could only mean that they were all inside; a fact that greatly displeased him. Shortly after, the man returned to water the engine and converse with one of its crew. It was only as the train began to pull away and the lone individual returned to the cabin that Dalton went back to his horse.

He mounted up and headed carefully down the hillside towards the railway track. The Union Pacific employee had disappeared and the train was steaming its way east. The hired gun was very tired after his long ride through the enervating heat, but deep inside of him a seething anger was building up. Something was not right down at the pumping station, and if any of his men were to blame, then they would suffer the torments of the damned. He had risked far too much to allow some half-baked gunhand the chance to jeopardize everything. His parley with the band of Lakota Sioux had been a terrifying experience, but had yielded the required result. He had secured the allies that he needed for the assault on the presidential train.

Tatum slammed the door behind him and glared impotently at the four men. Sarah still had a gun muzzle pressed against her skull, but her eyes blazed fire and her wits had obviously returned.

'I should have gunned you all down while I had the chance,' she somewhat implausibly stated.

'My, my. You're a real hellcat,' responded Forrest appreciatively, as he tightened his grip on her hair.

She winced with pain and stared at her father, as though willing the unarmed man to do something, anything. Tatum spread his arms wide to show that he did not represent a physical threat. His sole intention was to get the gun away from her head, so he used the only weapon that he possessed. Words.

'How on earth do you four really expect to kill the President of the United States? You've had all on handling this slip of a girl.'

Even the wounded Van Dorn ceased his moaning as he absorbed that.

'What the hell are you on about?' snarled the belligerent Forrest. His revolver had swung away from Sarah, but was now pointing directly at their accuser. 'We ain't here to kill anyone, are we?' He glanced incredulously at the others.

'So what *are* you doing here?' Tatum demanded.

It was then that Sarah found her tongue again. 'There's another man in charge, Pa. He left hours ago.'

At that moment the door behind Tatum swung open and Brett Dalton crossed the threshold.

'Yes, but I'm back now,' he remarked softly. His sharp eyes took in the scene before him. Van Dorn's shoulder wound. The carelessly discarded Henry rifle. Forrest's hand tightly intertwined in Sarah's hair. And most ominously, the blood on her face.

Shoving Tatum to one side, Dalton's eyes almost seemed to glaze over as he put the question.

'Who made her bleed?'

Disconcertingly, he didn't appear to be looking at anyone in particular, yet all four men felt suddenly apprehensive; none more so than Forrest, who immediately released his grip on the young woman.

'She shot Van Dorn with that long gun, for Christ's sake,' he protested. 'If she'd put us all down, where would you be without any back-up?'

'Probably better off, since you're all just worthless scum.' Dalton paused slightly, before repeating remorselessly, 'Who made her bleed?'

For all the baking summer heat, the apparent temperature in the cabin had plummeted. Forrest desperately peered around at his companions for support, but none was forthcoming. The fact that his revolver was already drawn gave him little comfort. Then, suddenly, his natural aggression returned and he thought, *The hell with it!*

To Dalton he stated, 'I had no choice. Either I hit her or shot her. Seeing how pretty she is and how bored we were, that would have seemed a waste.'

He leered over at the others, confident that his suggestive remark would attract their support. The other three didn't even smirk. They remained rigid, their collective gaze fixed on Brett Dalton. That individual's expression was like a mask, except for his eyes. They seemed to contain a lethal intensity, which completely entranced all of those in the cabin.

'I told you to stay clear of the lady.'

Those who witnessed it would afterwards affirm that they had never seen such speed in their lives. Only a fool or someone supremely confident would draw against a man already holding a six-shooter. Dalton's right hand moved so swiftly that the action was just a blur. Belatedly, Forrest realized that death was beckoning. He levelled his gun, but was just a split second too late. As the assassin's Colt crashed out, the ball caught Forrest in his heart and he was dead before hitting the floor.

With their ears ringing painfully, the five stunned onlookers regarded Dalton with a mixture of fear and awe. Seeing that one chamber was sufficient, he returned his revolver to its oiled belly holster.

Almost as an afterthought he remarked, 'Oh and you were right, railroad man. We *are* here to kill the President.'

'What on earth for?' croaked Tatum unsteadily.

'The best of all reasons. Money!'

CHAPTER SEVEN

By the time that Thad had finished his business in Julesburg's telegraph office his shamefaced assistant had returned. Jud was mortified that the individual whom he had earlier knocked out had managed to get clean away. In his eagerness to reach the storeroom, he had lost his eyebrows and some hair to the intolerable heat and was not a happy man. The saloon-cum-hotel had collapsed in on its own rudimentary foundations and was now just a smoking ruin. Everything in it was irrevocably lost, a fact guaranteed to displease the settlement's heavy drinkers.

'I hope you fared better,' Jud remarked hopefully.

'For better or worse, it's out of our hands for now,' Thad grimly responded. 'I telegraphed the marshal at North Platte, asking him to hold Grant's train there whenever it might arrive. I gave him my reasons, but I wouldn't bet a plugged nickel for his chances. The President is an ornery son of a bitch at the best of times. He may decide to just steam on through.'

'So what do we do?' Jud queried, quietly relieved that it wasn't his decision.

That had already made up his mind. 'We head for Fort

Sedgwick and see if there's any kind of garrison there. These good citizens of Julesburg have got at least one body to bury and I'm mighty sure they'll be glad to see the back of us.'

His companion was plainly puzzled. 'But there are soldiers on the train. Why do we need any more?'

'Think about it!' Thad hissed. 'This fellow Dalton is sure to know that and yet he's still proceeding. Which means that he is not worried and we should be. In such circumstances I am quite prepared to ride a few extra miles to recruit some soldier boys.'

Fort Sedgwick was an imposing yet unusual structure situated near the South Platte River. The walls must have been all of fifteen feet high, but they weren't made of wood or any form of building block. Constructed on the vast empty plains before the arrival of the railroad, it had required massive quantities of prairie marble and a prodigious amount of effort from the garrison's enlisted men.

The first signs were not encouraging. There were no sentries on the walls and both main gates were hanging open. There was an unmistakable aura of dereliction. The two men regarded each other with sinking hearts. It had been no easy task to get there. After the destruction that they had wrought in Julesburg, the liveryman had been very reluctant to rent them any horses or supply them with directions. It had required the production of Thad's Justice Department shield and a deal of threatening language. And all the while time was passing.

Thad cursed softly as they rode unchallenged through the gates. Then, unexpectedly, movement registered on his peripheral vision and he swung round in his saddle.

'And just who the devil are you two boyos?'

The accent was unmistakably Irish, just as the weapon aimed vaguely in their direction was unmistakably a Spencer carbine. The lawmen reined in and watched as a burly, blue-clad figure emerged from the nearest building. He was ruddy-faced, red-haired and belligerent. On each sleeve of his tunic there were three yellow chevrons, topped by three bars. The colour indicated that he belonged to a cavalry regiment.

Thad raised both hands in a placating gesture. 'Easy there, Sergeant. We're no threat to you, but we do need to see your commanding officer. Immediately.'

'Immediately, is it? Well it's *quartermaster* sergeant to you, mister. And this place might not look much now, but it's still army property. So I'll decide who you see and when.'

Thad's eyes glinted dangerously. He just didn't have time for all this. Keeping his hands in plain sight and away from any weapons, he motioned his horse slowly towards the soldier. That individual relaxed his stance, confident that he had established his superiority. Without warning, Thad dug in his heels hard and urged his mount forward. The animal leapt towards the startled cavalryman and struck him a glancing blow as it charged past.

Viciously tugging on the bit, the lawman dismounted before the beast had even stopped. He raced over to the prone and winded soldier and kicked the carbine out of reach. The man's revolver was securely tucked away in a flap holster and so presented no immediate threat.

'Don't ever point a gun at me again, *Sergeant*!'

Before he could say anything else there was a flurry of activity at the far side of the compound. Half a dozen blue-coated figures emerged from a building and ran towards them. Thankfully, one of them was quite obviously an officer. Thad withdrew the brass shield of office from his pocket and, holding it high, strode over to meet him. Mindful of what had just occurred, Jud also dismounted and stood close to the panting NCO.

The fresh-faced young officer regarded the unfamiliar shield with bewilderment.

'Just what is the meaning of this?' he demanded in a strangely high-pitched voice.

Maintaining steady eye contact, Thad stated his case. 'My name is Thaddeus McEvoy. This is Jud Parker. We both work for the Justice Department. I answer directly to US Attorney-General Williams.'

So far so good. The officer was wide-eyed and paying full attention.

'You may or may not know that President Grant is heading this way on a special train. I have reason to believe that there will be an attempt on his life.' Thad made no effort to lower his voice. He wanted every enlisted man in the post on side when they pulled out, including the quartermaster sergeant. As he continued, he heard that man stomping up behind him, no doubt shadowed by Jud. Then, gratifyingly, the officer impatiently waved him away and the threat abruptly receded.

'I have here a document that authorizes me to requisition anything and anybody that I see fit.' With that he handed the oilskin folder over and allowed its recipient time to read it.

The soldier blinked repeatedly as he digested Thad's really quite extraordinary powers. Sweat poured down his face and it wasn't all due to the summer heat. He swallowed and eventually asked a question. 'Why do you need our help? Surely President Grant already has an army escort?'

'Oh, yeah. General Sherman has provided him with a sizeable detachment equipped with Trapdoor Springfields, but I don't think that that's going to be enough.' Gesturing vaguely towards the west, Thad continued, 'There is a very dangerous man on the loose out there who already knows exactly what he's up against.' Disconcertingly, he suddenly laughed and favoured the officer with a genuine smile before adding: 'Like it or not, you are working for me now, or I will have your commission, Lieutenant. . . ?'

The young man had the good grace to accept the inevitable. Folding and returning the justice man's bona fides, he replied, 'Galloway, sir. Lieutenant Frederick Galloway of the Fifth Cavalry. My men and I are currently assigned to the Department of the Platte.'

'Good, good,' Thad responded impatiently. 'But how many of you are there?'

Galloway's features registered embarrassment. 'Not as many as you might like, Mr McEvoy. Fort Sedgwick no longer has a garrison. If the army needs to chase redskins out here now, they just use the railroad to move troops about. I have Quartermaster Sergeant O'Halloran and thirty men. We are removing anything of value from the fort before it is abandoned.'

So that was it! The Justice Department had suddenly acquired an army of thirty-two bluecoats. Thad could only pray to God that it would be enough.

A short while later thirty-four men rode out of Fort Sedgwick in the traditional column-of-twos formation. The enlisted men all carried with them an air of anticipation, for this was no routine assignment. Their lives normally consisted of boredom and hardship; fatigues and endless guard duty on the frontier, enlivened by patrols and the occasional moment of paralyzing fear. The sudden arrival of two civilians had changed all that. Now they were setting out on a grand mission to find and protect the President of the United States. And, even better, they had seen Patrick O'Halloran unceremoniously bounced into the dust.

'You'd better not be after trying anything like that again, *Mister* Justice Department Man, *sir*!' The quarter-master sergeant regarded the lawman through narrowed eyes as they jogged along next to each other. In his experience, military and civilian authorities made a bad combination and this one had certainly got off to a bad start.

'Maybe I was a bit rough on you,' McEvoy allowed. 'But time is short and needs must. Besides, you Irish are known for taking hard knocks in your stride.'

'And ain't that the truth?' O'Halloran responded with the makings of a smile.

'So what do I call you, without always having to fight you?' Thad enquired. 'By the time I call out, "Watch out, Quartermaster Sergeant O'Halloran" you could be stone dead from a Sioux arrow.'

The NCO chuckled. He was actually beginning to take a shine to this lawman.

'Well, seeing as you appear to outrank me, I reckon "Sergeant" will do.'

Thad reached over for a vigorous shake of hands. That brief contact was enough to cement an understanding of sorts and he replied, 'Very well, Sergeant. Now, you'll have to excuse me while I parley with your officer. He really needs to know what he's getting himself into.' He urged his horse to greater speed and overhauled the young lieutenant. That man was looking around edgily, as though expecting to be attacked at any moment.

'It's not us they're after, Lieutenant,' Thad remarked lightly. 'Grant's train is the target, wherever the hell that is right now.'

The young man released a deep sigh and coloured slightly. 'Sorry, sir. Only I'm new to all this. This is my first posting out West and I haven't even seen any hostile Indians yet.'

'And hopefully you won't,' replied Thad, wondering at the same time whether the lieutenant had just uttered a prophetic statement. 'It's white men that we're after and it is only fair that you should know my intentions. I'm not a religious man, but I hope and pray that Grant's train is still well to the east of us. Even if he received my warning, he may or may not have chosen to heed it. To save time, I propose to ride directly to the town of Sydney, rather than shadow the track. We'll keep going until the light has gone and we have to camp for the night, but it's still going to be late morning before we get there. I believe that any ambuscade will take place further west, well away from all settlements.'

The young officer regarded him curiously. 'What do you know of the man that we're after?'

Thad's features perceptibly hardened. As he spoke, there was a chillingly matter-of-fact edge to his tone.

'I have never seen him. His name is Dalton and he is a professional assassin for hire. He has a gang of gun thugs with him, but they've been whittled down some. Jud and I paroled five of them to Jesus in Julesburg this very morning.'

Galloway's jaw dropped. In his short time on active service, he had not actually seen any action. Yet here he was in company with a man fresh from a great deal of bloodletting. The harsh reality of the situation suddenly dawned on him. He was now part of some deadly game of cat and mouse that made his laborious task in Fort Sedgwick seem somehow suddenly very appealing.

Total darkness on the plains came very late at that time of year. Even at ten o'clock it was still possible to make out the solitary rider as he approached the pumping station. He was a long way off and moving slowly, as though all was not well with him.

'And he's not the only one out there,' Nelson asserted nervously. 'There's someone up in those hills watching this place.'

'That'll be the Lakota,' Dalton responded blandly. 'I know about them. It's this one I'm interested in.'

'Redskins!' bleated Van Dorn plaintively. His shoulder had been bandaged, but he was still in a great deal of pain. The prospect of an Indian attack appalled him. 'I thought you weren't supposed to be able to see those devils.'

'Unless they want you to,' Dalton retorted. 'Since I invited them here, they are probably just letting me know that they have arrived.'

That information was just too much for the men in the cabin. Brad Taylor leapt to his feet, face flushed and angry.

'We're working for you, Mr Dalton, and you're like greased lightning with that belly gun, but if you want us to do a proper job for you it's time you told us just what the hell is going on!'

Dalton viewed him through narrowed eyes. He was deciding whether it was the right opportunity and came to the conclusion that, yes it was. He had plenty of time before their lone visitor arrived. So, without any preamble, he launched straight into the astounding plan.

'President Grant is riding the rails to re-election in a special train. Conveniently for us it is festooned in flags and banners, so our friends up there won't miss it.'

'*Friends*!' spat Nelson. 'They're just a bunch of murdering savages.'

'And you're not?' countered their leader scornfully. 'They're doing it to survive. What's your excuse?'

Taylor, the more thoughtful of the gunmen, was puzzled. 'But what has attracted them to attack this particular train? Killing the Great White Father would be the end of them. The army would never let up.'

Dalton favoured him with a cold smile. 'Because someone told them that the special passenger was actually a certain Columbus Delano, Secretary of the Interior. He is the man behind the hated reservation system and he just happens to support the slaughter of all the buffalo. They were also told that there are many rifles and much ammunition just for the taking. What they weren't told was that they would have to take them from the soldiers to whom they'd been issued.'

'Clever,' allowed Taylor. 'Very clever.'

'I know,' replied Dalton without any sign of smugness. 'And we are going to make sure it can't fail. With the help of this railroad man, we will take over the engine and turn Grant into a sitting duck. Even if his escort can handle the

Lakota, they won't be expecting trouble from us.'

He felt a glow of satisfaction at the prospect of such success and the money that it would bring him, until he encountered Sarah's unblinking gaze. Its sheer intensity was disconcerting, even for him. It contained a mixture of scorn and loathing and yet something else besides. Whatever that 'something else' was, it was enough to make him decide to vacate the cabin. For some strange reason, what she thought of him seemed to matter.

'Sweet Jesus, it's Baker!' exclaimed Taylor with genuine surprise. 'Why's he all on his lonesome?'

Dalton and his two remaining able-bodied men were standing in the gathering gloom as their visitor slowly walked his horse up to them. The assassin did not trouble to answer, as he had already made the obvious assumption and didn't relish the likely consequences. Still, it was worth hearing what the oaf had to say.

Baker painfully reined in before them and just sat his horse in silence. Then, as Taylor advanced to help him, he suddenly toppled sideways out of the saddle. Taylor just managed to catch him before he crashed to the hard earth.

'Water,' he croaked through parched lips.

As Nelson turned away to get a canteen, Dalton stated bluntly, 'You can have all the damned water you want, once you've told me what happened.'

'He'd talk a whole lot faster after some water, you bastard,' muttered Nelson under his breath.

Baker, hatless and sun-blistered, groaned feebly and struggled to produce some words. Even in the bad light, the huge bruise on his forehead was plain to see.

'All five ... dead as a wagon tyre. Those law dogs torched the saloon and killed everyone in it. Women, children, babies an' all.'

Dalton felt an unaccustomed shock flow through him. Even allowing for Baker's undoubted exaggeration, it was still turning out to be a day for surprises. The lawmen had to be very good at their jobs to wreak such havoc. Turning away dismissively, he drifted over towards the railroad track. The night air was oppressive and did nothing to improve his mood. He felt desperately weary, but knew that he had to think things through. For in truth, he was under almost intolerable pressure. The lack of knowledge as to just when Grant's train would arrive was partly responsible. He couldn't risk connecting to the telegraph wires in case any messages were intercepted by the unusually persistent lawmen. And just where the hell were they at that moment? It was an important consideration now that he and his men were committed to remaining at the Barklam's water stop.

That name suddenly brought thoughts of the young lady flooding into his head. It had been a bad call killing Forrest, but the sight of blood on her lovely face had aroused a burning rage within him.

'Why did you kill that horrible man?'

The hushed and uncannily timed question came from behind and to the side of him and caused Dalton momentary alarm. How had she managed to get so close? It was a sign of just how tired he was. Slowly turning, he was able to make out her delectable features as she stared earnestly up at him.

'Because he disobeyed my orders. I told them all to stay away from you.' That was only part of it, but he couldn't tell her the main reason. 'It made them realize that my intentions were serious. Besides,' he added lightly and with a smile, '*you* shot Van Dorn first.'

'I only winged him,' she corrected, before snorting disdainfully. 'Anyway, he deserved it and what's more he doesn't sound anything like a Dutchman to me.'

'A lot of people aren't what they seem,' the gunman answered cryptically.

'But you must be,' she decided bleakly. 'If you are intending to murder your president for money.'

From over by the cabin there were scuffling sounds. Dalton glanced over sharply, but relaxed when he realized that it was only Nelson helping Baker over to the water. 'He did well to find us here,' he remarked quietly, before returning his attention to the girl. Christ, but she had lovely eyes!

'Grant is not my president,' he blurted out. 'Besides, titles mean nothing to me. He is just a man like any other. Do you know how many thousands of his own men that he slaughtered in Virginia, throwing them needlessly against Lee's fortifications?'

Sarah remained silent. What could she say to an accusation like that? She knew nothing of war.

'What you need to think about is that pa of yours,' Dalton continued. 'He's got the mark of a brave man and brave men get themselves killed. When that train arrives, I don't want any heroics. You tell him that, huh? He does exactly what I say and I promise that neither of you will get hurt.'

Sarah stared up at his dark features. There was something chillingly reprehensible about the man but, as when she first met him, she felt strangely drawn to him. 'I will do my best,' she stated simply, before turning away and returning to the cabin and her anxious father.

'Let's hope that is good enough,' Dalton murmured into the darkness as he in turn headed for the horses. His body urgently craved sleep, but Baker's solitary arrival had changed things. If those damned lawmen were still dogging his trail, then they needed to be given a little something extra to keep them occupied.

As Dalton reluctantly saddled his horse, Brad Taylor materialized through the gloom to enquire as to his intentions. That man appeared to possess the most intelligence in his much-reduced gang, so he took the trouble to explain his actions.

'Shouldn't take me long,' he concluded. 'But if you hear any shooting, you'll know that they didn't take to their additional duties and all bets are off.'

'Fair enough,' Taylor replied shortly. He didn't need telling just how cheap life could be on the frontier.

CHAPTER EIGHT

U.S. (Unconditional Surrender, as he was known in the war) Grant cautiously opened his eyes and groaned. He was known to enjoy a drink and the previous night, the good citizens of North Platte, Nebraska, had shamelessly plied him with alcohol and good food. It was not every day that a serving president arrived in town and they had fully intended to make the best of it.

Closing his eyes, he shifted position on the cot in his private sleeping quarters. Then he heard voices outside and even on the roof as the soldiers went about their morning routine.

'That's it,' he decided ruefully. 'If they're up, then I'm up. Once a soldier, always a soldier.'

A short while later the President, clad in a sober frock-coat, was drinking strong coffee in the day carriage. Secretary Delano entered, showing no signs of any ill-effects from the previous night.

'Good morning, Mr President,' he announced brightly.

' 'Morning, Columbus,' Grant managed. His head was aching abominably and he really didn't want company. Then again, the pain was telling him that he'd definitely had enough of North Platte. With an effort he asked, 'Where are we steaming off for today, pray tell?'

As expected, the Secretary of the Interior had all the answers. 'Julesburg, Colorado first. We won't be there long. By all accounts it has a grim history and hasn't improved with time. Then on to Sydney, Nebraska for a little glad-handing. After that across the border into Wyoming and ending the day in Cheyenne. Big town. Should be good for a rousing speech.'

The President groaned. Just at that moment, making any kind of speech was the last thing that he felt like. 'And what about the threat of bloody violence to my person? Any news on that?'

'Nothing at all,' reported Delano. 'But that doesn't make it less real.'

Grant snorted. For a brief instant he actually wished for some incident to befall them. Something, anything, just to interrupt the interminable round of speechmaking. If nothing else, news of the President personally braving danger had to be good for a few votes. Then breakfast was announced and the moment was gone. Or so he thought!

Quartermaster Sergeant O'Halloran none too gently booted the slumbering troopers awake. Bugle calls had been strictly forbidden in what was very possibly enemy territory. Dawn was barely upon them, but Thad McEvoy was keen to be off and for the foreseeable future his word was law. The column of twos had managed to cover about ten miles the previous night, leaving them with roughly twenty more to reach Sydney. In such weather a cold camp was no hardship, but they all rode off regretting the lack of that first mug of coffee.

They had barely a couple of miles left to travel when two unrelated things occurred. A burst of whistling from a steam engine was plainly audible in the distance, and a single gunshot rang out. A horse abruptly reared up in agony, throwing its rider. The trooper fell heavily on the sun-baked ground and lay still.

'Dismount,' O'Halloran yelled superfluously.

The designated horse-holders took four mounts each. The remaining twenty-one men formed up in a skirmish line in front of their officer and ranking NCO and then dropped down on to the grass.

'Neatly done,' commented Jud admiringly, as he and Thad remained in the rear. It made sense to let the cavalry get on about its business.

'Watch for smoke,' bellowed the sergeant. At that precise moment another projectile ploughed into the earth just beyond the horse herd. A diminutive, sulphurous cloud appeared above a small rise some 200 yards away.

'Corporal Deacon's squad, fire for effect,' O'Halloran commanded.

It was plain to see who was really in charge of the detachment. Seven carbines crashed out in unison. Dust was kicked up at the correct range, but since their assailant was hidden none of the bullets penetrated flesh.

'What are their numbers, Sergeant?' demanded Galloway, who was keen to demonstrate some semblance of command.

O'Halloran ran a meaty hand over his grizzled features and murmured to himself, 'God save us from shavetails.' Aloud, he replied, 'That kind of depends on what their intentions are, sir. If they are just trying to slow us up, well then one man is as good as an army. On the other hand, if it's redskins out there they might be looking to draw us in for a repeat of the Fetterman massacre.'

The lieutenant visibly paled at such a scenario and appeared to be lost for words, but Thad had heard enough. An uneasy assumption was forming in his mind that suggested a connection with their current predicament and their position relative to the rail track. It was time to force events.

'Mr Galloway, I suspect that this is connected to our pursuit. I suggest you flush out these bushwhackers, so that we can be on our way.'

The young officer blinked and then, in a vain attempt at face-saving, called over to his subordinate. 'I believe that we should flush them out, Sergeant O'Halloran. You may proceed.'

'Yes, sir. Thank you, sir.' The NCO's face was a picture, but he had sense enough not to push it. Then there was another gunshot and a horse-holder yelped with pain. He had been struck in the left arm, but had gamely clung on to all the reins in his charge.

'Deacon,' yelled O'Halloran. 'Your squad, independent fire.' He then detailed the two remaining squads to advance on either flank. As sustained fire rattled out those men leapt to their feet and moved swiftly forward. If it were an ambush, then they would soon find out.

The two lawmen watched as the soldiers approached the rise. Suddenly, as if from nowhere, a painted warrior rose up into view astride a pony. Screaming out some form of challenge, that individual fired once for effect, before racing off to the west. All of the troopers returned fire, but a man on a speeding horse makes for a difficult target and every bullet missed its mark.

'No massacre today, sir,' reported O'Halloran on his return. His officer's features tightened at the veiled sarcasm and boded ill for the future. It was never wise to upset an officer, however junior he might be. The situation was not helped by Thad who, beset with impatience, was no longer bothered with the proprieties.

'See to your wounded and saddle up, Sergeant. We're for Sydney at all speed and I just hope that we're in time!'

The special train pulled into Sydney, Nebraska in a swirl of flags and superheated steam. Grant was adjusting his cravat, prior to stepping out on the open platform for some suitably presidential posturing. Alongside the track a curious crowd was forming, drawn by the shrill whistle. Yet, puzzlingly, they were also pointing and staring off into the distance.

The carriage door opened and Captain Beauchamp strode in. He was a young, good-looking officer with impressive sideburns, who had been given command of the presidential detail by General Sherman himself. Years before, as a newly commissioned second lieutenant, he had come to his commanding general's attention during the Union Army's march through Georgia. He had proved himself adept at both administration and battlefield command. Even in the vastly smaller post-war army, he was obviously destined for greater things. Now, although not easily spooked, the concern on his face was plain to see.

'Gunfire, Mr President. Off to the south-east.'

At that moment, and with the door still open, there was the unmistakable sound of volley fire. The captain was under no illusions as to his duty. 'I think we should get out of here, now, sir. While we still have steam pressure.'

Grant bristled with annoyance. He had already cut short the visit to Julesburg that morning, mainly because there had been little apparent reason to linger. The town's largest saloon was a smoking ruin and the low-life residents seemed to have little interest in anything beyond the urgent necessity of replacing their destroyed joy juice. Even as his train had pulled away from the Union Pacific depot, the President had been trying to get to grips with a report that the disastrous blaze had actually been started by an agent of the Justice Department. Now, however, he had other things on his mind.

'It just doesn't sit well with me to cut and run, Captain.'

That officer was acutely aware of the President's outstanding military credentials.

'I can understand that, sir, but under the circumstances I think it would be for the best. It's not just you as an individual that I am responsible for. It's also the office of president and what that represents.'

As if to punctuate that remark there was another burst of firing and Secretary Delano arrived through the other door.

'Well said, Captain. Now get this train moving!' To Grant he stated, 'You're not fighting a war now. You're on a re-election campaign. We can't just sit around waiting to be attacked, Mr President. I'm told that we can take on water at a pumping station near Lodgepole Creek, so there's no need to remain here.'

The army officer stood his ground without comment. He knew exactly where his orders came from. Grant fixed his gaze on him and reluctantly nodded his assent. 'See to it, Captain Beauchamp.'

That man saluted, left the cabin and began bellowing out commands.

'He's a good officer,' Grant commented quietly. 'I can see why Sherman picked him for this trip.'

Shortly after, the carriage shuddered as the engine took up the strain and began to pull them out of Sydney. The townsfolk peered up at the country's departing leader and shook their heads in disbelief. It occurred to more than one of them that the former commanding general was not showing a great deal of courage under fire that day. Inside the plush carriage that individual shook his head regretfully.

'I don't think there'll be many votes coming my way from this place.'

The column of soldiers swept into Sydney at speed. There were plenty of citizens on the main street and their apprehension was obvious. Picking one likely fellow, Thad called over to him.

'We heard a steam whistle. What news of the President's train?'

The man scornfully spat a stream of tobacco juice into the dust. 'That lily-livered bastard pulled out as soon as the shooting started. He won't be getting my vote and that's for sure. Say, what was that ruckus anyhow?'

'God damn it to hell,' snarled Thad in exasperation. Completely ignoring the aggrieved citizen, he called over to Jud. 'Tell Galloway to leave his wounded here and be ready to move out. I'm going to telegraph Cheyenne to hold the train if it gets there. It's no coincidence that that redskin jumped us. There are probably more of them dotted about to cover plenty of country. Somebody's got them riled up and that's no error!'

Less than twenty minutes later the column was on its way again, only this time in hot pursuit. The wounded trooper had been left with the local sawbones, so they were no longer a horse short. The man who had taken a heavy tumble had recovered and was gamely riding along. Every single enlisted man seemed to have realized the urgency of their mission, so there were no shirkers or malingerers.

'The engine will have to take on water at a pumping station just over the border,' Thad bellowed to the lieutenant over the pounding of hoofs. 'It's run by a man and his daughter and there's no telegraph station there.'

Galloway nodded but maintained a brooding silence. Things were happening too fast for the young officer. A civilian had usurped his position and in his opinion the events so far hadn't proved conclusively that there was any direct threat to the President's train. Yet if he had been able to obtain a bird's-eye view of the water stop, all of his doubts would have vanished in an instant.

Brett Dalton carefully placed a kerchief on the iron rail and then pressed his ear to it. Even through the material, he could feel the fierce heat absorbed from the midday sun. There was something else as well and it made him smile. A vibration that could mean only one thing. Since there were no scheduled trains due, it had to signify the imminent arrival of the President of the United States.

He clambered to his feet, drew his Colt and fired twice. That was the signal to alert the Lakota war party up in the hills. His own men looked up expectantly. Three of them were lounging in the shade of the elevated water tank, along with a stony-faced Tatum Barklam. His daughter remained in the cabin under the watchful eye of the wounded Van Dorn. This time her hands were tied and there was no sign of the Henry rifle.

Already that morning Tatum had been forced into the charade of appearing relaxed and untroubled before the crew of the Cheyenne train. Now it appeared that his greatest test was imminent. And yet, how could he just stand by whilst President Grant was gunned down by hired killers? His guts were churning relentlessly from the torturous anxiety. If only he could get Sarah away from that bastard in the cabin!

Dalton strode vigorously towards them. His terrible weariness of the previous night had vanished. This was to be his big payday. Nothing could ever surpass this. His searching eyes took in the scene before him and he knew exactly what was required.

'Baker, you ain't yourself yet. Lead the horses round the back of the cabin again and keep them there. We don't want anyone on that train getting suspicious. Taylor, you and me will follow Barklam over to the train, as though we are just innocent passengers not realizing who's on board. We'll carry our bedrolls with our rifles inside.'

The gunman suddenly stopped and stared long and hard at Tatum. 'When I look at your face, railroad man, I see something I don't like. So let me tell you this one time only. Anything goes wrong, any little thing at all and the girl's dead meat. Your fault, my fault, anybody's fault, it doesn't matter to me. You understand me, railroad man?'

Tatum Barklam returned the stare. He was seething with anger and loathing, but at the end of the day he knew that he simply had no choice. Very slowly, he nodded his head.

Dalton grunted. 'Say it!'

Tatum drew in a deep breath and replied through gritted teeth. 'I understand.'

A smile flitted across Dalton's features, which totally failed to reach his eyes. 'Well now, that wasn't too hard, was it?'

With that, he turned away and ambled over towards his bedroll. He thanked Christ that he'd got Barklam's measure, because he knew in his heart that in reality he just could not harm Sarah, no matter what the provocation. Van Dorn had actually been instructed to stay with the young woman to ensure that no harm came to her, on pain of death.

Nelson's reedy voice called out, 'I can see the train, boss. It sure does look pretty with all those flags and such.'

'It begins, then,' remarked the hired gun with remarkable composure. 'Nelson, you stay out of the way until we've taken the engine. If we should get into trouble, give us covering fire. Once the Lakota come barrelling down that hillside, nobody will give a damn about us.' As if to punctuate that remark, a sustained whistle shrieked out a short way down the rails. 'Looks like this is it, boys. Remember what I told you, railroad man!'

Captain Jonas Beauchamp was with ten of his men in the carriage behind the engine tender. As the whistle blew long and hard, he stepped out on to the open platform followed by a sergeant. As his keen eyes scrutinized the surroundings he suddenly felt strangely uneasy. It was certainly a godforsaken, sun-blasted spot in which to spend one's life. There wasn't another human being for miles around. It was a pity that they had to stop to take on water, but they just couldn't risk allowing the engine to overheat. As the presidential train drew closer, three men emerged from the shade of the huge water tank. One was wearing the overalls of a Union Pacific employee, whilst the others were carrying bedrolls and appeared to be ill-informed potential passengers. Then again, considered the captain, if that was what they were, then how had they got to such an isolated spot in the first place? There were no horses picketed near by and the station did not possess a stable. Some sixth sense nibbled away at him like an itch and so he turned to the NCO.

'Tell your men to stand to, Sergeant. I want them outside as soon as we stop.'

As the other man returned inside, Beauchamp snorted to himself. He was being over cautious and he knew it. What possible threat could two men be to the train? He had soldiers on the roof of all the carriages and further back there was another railroad car filled with blue-coated infantry. As the locomotive slowed to a halt by the water tank, the man in overalls waved up at the engineer and the captain stepped aside to allow his men access to the steps.

'It'll do them no harm to get some air,' he considered. 'And who knows, they might even get a glimpse of Barklam's daughter who, according to the fireman, is supposed to be quite a beauty.'

CHAPTER NINE

The three men moved steadily towards the massive, panting engine, but there was nothing companionable about their progress. The Union Pacific employee felt as though there was a tight band constricting his chest. He longed to scream out a warning to the watching crew and then run like hell, but of course he could do no such thing. His daughter's life was simply too precious.

'Hi there, Tatum. Ben said you'd been down with the cramps. If you ask me you still don't look so good.' The engineer had obviously spoken with the crew of the previous day's eastbound train and was keen to explore the gossip.

Before any strained reply could be offered, Brett Dalton hustled forward.

'Howdy, friend. Me and my partner here are seeking passage to Cheyenne. Might you have any spare seats?'

At that moment there came the clomping of heavy boots and for no apparent reason a file of infantry began to descend from the nearest carriage. The assassin's plan to simply take over the engine unopposed was suddenly in tatters. He had to think on his feet and fast. Abruptly switching his attention to the fireman, he innocently asked, 'Do you know how to drive this marvellous machine?'

That man, his face covered in soot and sweat, favoured him with a simple smile. 'Sure can, mister.' Glancing nervously at the burly engineer, he added, 'There's nothing to it really.'

Dalton, gripping his Winchester inside the bedroll, replied, 'Well that's hard luck for you,' and squeezed the trigger.

There was a muffled crash and blood gushed from the fireman's chest as he fell back against the tender. For a brief moment everyone seemed to be frozen in time. Then all hell broke loose. Throwing his bedroll up into the cab, the gunfighter yelled at Taylor, 'Blast the driver!'

Drawing his Colt with breathtaking speed, Dalton next opened up on the startled soldiers. Those men were all armed and on their feet, but they might as well have been mere sitting ducks. Having been ordered to 'stand to', they had unslung their single-shot breech-loaders, but were congregated near the carriage steps, completely unprepared for violent action. In a blaze of rapid firing, Dalton emptied his revolver and every ball struck flesh and blood. Miraculously, there were no misfires. Taylor, having shot the engineer in the back of his head as he tried to flee, also dumped his rifle and added to the chaos by replicating his leader's actions.

Dalton holstered his empty belt gun and leapt up into the bloodstained cab. 'Nelson,' he bellowed out, 'kill anybody holding a gun.'

That individual opened up a rapid fire on the remaining soldiers before switching his attention to those sitting on the nearest carriage roof, thereby completing the rout. He was momentarily aware of Tatum Barklam dashing past his line of sight but, knowing him to be unarmed, chose to ignore him.

Captain Beauchamp was momentarily stunned. The air was abruptly filled with agonized screams. Without any prior warning his men were collapsing in a welter of blood and gore. Well-handled revolvers at close range had all but wiped them out. Making a conscious effort, he drew his service revolver from its flap holster and yelled at his sergeant, 'Get more men up here, now!'

At that moment and unbeknown to the captain, the hillside on the far side of the train erupted into vivid life. Scores of half-naked, garishly daubed warriors galloped down towards the track. They were brandishing a variety of weapons and shrieking like demented demons. For those unused to fighting the Plains Indians, the overall effect was mind-numbingly terrifying.

In the rearmost carriage Columbus Delano swept the thick curtain aside and peered out at the advancing horde. His blood ran cold as his orderly mind grasped the awful reality of the situation.

'Sweet Jesus!' he exclaimed. 'Where the hell are the soldiers?' His bowels had suddenly turned to mush and he felt a very real need to use the privy.

'Do you know how to use one of these?' Grant was sitting at his mahogany desk, calmly checking the chambers of a brace of gleaming Navy Colts. They had been presented to the President and war hero by a representative of the Colt Armory in Hartford, Connecticut.

'I've never fired a gun in my life,' cried Delano. He

appeared aghast that the President should even consider such action.

'Well, keep out of my goddamned way, then,' Grant snarled back. His features registered the steely determination that had stood him in such good stead during the War Between the States.

Dalton dragged the rifle from his bedroll and levered a cartridge into the firing chamber. Taylor, having emptied his own revolver, had joined him up in the cab. With most of the soldiers either dead or crawling off down the side of the track, he felt the heady elation of success.

'Hot dang! We did it, boss,' he yelled delightedly.

'We've done nothing yet,' returned the other man. 'Grant's still alive.'

'So what do we do next?'

'Hold this engine and let the Lakota do their part. With us here, this train is going nowhere.' With that, Dalton grabbed his revolver and pushed out the lug situated on the side of the barrel, which he was then able to remove. Replacing the empty cylinder with a fresh one from his pocket was a much swifter way to reload the weapon. Taylor copied his actions and soon the two men were reloaded and ready for whatever came their way.

Jonas Beauchamp was on the point of attempting to rescue some of his wounded men when his sergeant appeared next to him.

'We've got Indian trouble, sir. Lots of it!' He pulled his captain over to the far window.

'Christ almighty!' the officer exclaimed. 'Where did they come from?'

Rapidly he considered his priorities. His overwhelming

responsibility was to protect the life of the President. The greatest threat to that was the sudden appearance of the Lakota war party. The murderous white renegades in the engine would just have to wait, as would the injured enlisted men. Commanding the NCO to follow, Beauchamp raced off down the carriage. He threw open the door and leapt across the gap to the next one. Inside that he found roughly twenty more infantrymen milling about in total confusion. The white-faced corporal in charge appeared to be frozen with indecision.

'All you men on this side of the carriage, smash those windows and fire at will. Sergeant, get outside and take charge of whoever's on the roofs. The rest of you, follow me at the double.'

The captain pounded down the central aisle, heading for the next carriage. His positive commands had an immediate effect. Broken glass tumbled down to the side of the track and rapid fire opened up on the charging horsemen. Now, followed by a file of infantry, he hurtled on into the next carriage. This one held a kitchen and quarters for various servants. Beauchamp was appalled to find a fire burning away lustily in an iron cooking range. A coloured valet wearing a well-brushed frock-coat was kneeling before it, so as to keep below the window line.

'Put that bloody fire out,' roared the captain. 'We're under attack.'

As if to emphasize that fact, the nearest window shattered and a soldier howled in pain. Yet there was just no time to check on the man or observe that his order was carried out. The relentless rifle fire from the soldiers' carriage was having the unforeseen effect of channelling the warriors over towards a less well-defended part of the train:

namely the rear carriage containing President Grant.

Rushing past the terrified servants, the soldiers moved on to the next carriage containing the various secretaries and administration staff. As they reached the open platform a rifle crashed out above them. Glancing up, Beauchamp glimpsed a blue-clad figure reloading his Springfield.

'Well done, soldier,' he called out. 'Keep firing at those bastards.'

He then detailed two men to remain on the platform to support their comrade's fire. The whooping horsemen were by now barely fifty yards away, heading directly for the rear of the train, but unbeknown to him another group was already there. Bursting in amongst the President's staff, the captain dispensed with all deference.

'If any of you sons of bitches have got guns, use them. This is life and death!'

From further down the train he heard the distinctive, muted low boom of a Colt Navy. The hairs stood up on the back of his neck as he realized just what that signified.

For the first time in over seven long years Ulysses Grant felt the rush of adrenaline through his system. This was something that he understood. No meaningless wrangling with Congress or endless boring meetings, just a bunch of men trying their level best to kill him. With a Colt in each hand he smashed out the window glass and knelt down on the thick carpet. Secretary Delano had already shown his true colours by fleeing into the next carriage.

'God save me from misfires,' muttered the President as he drew a careful bead on the nearest warrior. At such range, windage and elevation had little to do with it and his aim was true. The revolver bucked satisfyingly in his hand as his stricken enemy crashed to the ground and then straight under the hoofs of the following horse. Grunting with satisfaction, Grant raised the barrel of the Colt to shake out the remains of the percussion cap before cocking it again. It suddenly occurred to him that he was completely alone and yet the fact did not worry him one little bit.

A group of warriors swept around the end of the rearmost carriage and leapt from their ponies. There was a disconcerting amount of gunfire from further down the line of wooden boxes on wheels, but back here there was no sign of any of the bluecoats. If they could force entry at this undefended point, then they could sweep right through the strange boxes until they reached the 'Iron Horse' itself. Their plans after that were somewhat hazy. No Lakota had ever before taken possession of such an awesome beast.

The first axe-wielding warrior bounded up the steps on to the platform, kicked down the door and rushed into the opulent carriage. At first glance it appeared to be completely deserted. Then, from behind an overturned mahogany desk at the far end, a heavily bearded white man appeared. He had a murderous glint in his eyes and held a levelled revolver. With a speed born of desperation, the Lakota flung himself forward, but in his heart he already knew that it was too late.

Don't ever scare. If you scare, you're dead! Those words, uttered by an old Indian fighter many years earlier, resounded in Grant's mind as he waited for the first redskin to burst into the carriage. He had tipped over his solid mahogany desk and was comforted by the knowledge that it was most definitely proof against any weapons that the Indians might possess. The President was also well aware that if enough of them got into the carriage at once they could overwhelm him and he would never experience his second term or, indeed, anything else. Perversely, that thought served only to bolster his determination. Then the door smashed open and the first painted savage rushed in, peering eagerly around for a victim.

Rising up from behind the desk, Grant fired at point-blank range. The .36-calibre ball caught the warrior square in his chest, stopping him in his tracks. Yet even as that man's life was snuffed out, another adrenaline-fuelled Lakota took his place. As the heady smell of sulphur wafted up into his nostrils, the solitary white man aimed his left-hand Colt at the threshold and fired. That ball carved a bloody furrow through his assailant's skull before careering off into the distance. With blood and brain-matter flowing over his face, the Lakota was dead on his feet, but the desperate momentum of those following him propelled him further into the carriage.

Remaining calm, Grant pointed both revolvers at the ceiling and cocked them. Small shards of copper dropped out of the mechanisms. He had nine chambers remaining. The Lakotas were using their stricken comrade as a screen. So, although unable to open fire, they were managing to swell their numbers. Dropping to his knees, so that only his upper body was visible behind the solid barricade, their opponent fired both revolvers.

In the enclosed space the brutal noise made his ears ring painfully. Both balls had drawn blood and fresh screams rent the smoke-filled atmosphere. Yet one of his victims had only been winged and was coming on again. Grant's heart was thumping rapidly. This was bloody work and in truth he was probably past his prime. He now had seven chambers remaining.

With manically staring eyes, the painted warrior closed in with a tomahawk raised for the kill. Again the embattled President cocked his weapons. He was aware of other Indians moving in around their wounded comrade and was struck by the awful realization that he would only get one more volley. As the axe head neared its mark, he again squeezed both triggers. The left-hand Colt belched forth death and the already wounded Lakota slewed sideways, his head crashing into window glass. The other revolver merely uttered a feeble pop. Misfire!

With exultant cries the remaining warriors moved in for the kill. One of them opened fire with an old Spencer, but the heavy ball slammed harmlessly into the thick mahogany. Then the forward door abruptly burst open and Captain Beauchamp entered the carriage. Sizing up the situation immediately, he leapt behind the desk next to the President and opened up with his Colt Army. The large-calibre revolver crashed out with comforting power. The .44-calibre ball struck their nearest assailant just above the bridge of his nose and shattered his skull.

As unprotected soldiers began to file into the carriage, those Indians with rifles returned fire. The first bluecoat crumpled to the floor, but the next fired his rifle and moved off to the side. More men surged into the compartment, firing on the move. The suddenly cramped space became a living nightmare of noise and smoke. Blood splashed over the opulent fittings as, with practised speed, the infantrymen crammed cartridges into the breeches of their Springfields. They blasted out bullet after bullet until the remaining Lakotas could take no more. Realizing that they had missed their chance, and dismayed by their losses, the Indians fled from the carriage, but remained outside firing their rifles at anyone who moved.

'By Christ, you cut that fine, Captain,' remarked the President, whose relief was plain to see. He was sweating profusely and heavily smudged with black powder.

'My apologies, sir. I got here as soon as I could.' As his men kept up a steady fusillade, he pulled the President down lower, until they were both squatting behind the desk. Staring directly at his commander-in-chief with deep concern, he stated, 'I believe that this is not just a random Indian raid. There are white men involved and they have taken control of the engine.'

Grant took his meaning immediately. 'So that justice man, McEvoy, had the right of it.'

Beauchamp nodded grimly. 'It would appear so, Mr President. And I don't think that I have enough men here to drive them all off. With your permission, I need to go back up the train and see just what is occurring.'

'You have it, young man,' Grant replied firmly. 'There are enough of us to hold this carriage.'

Their eyes remained locked for a few more seconds, then the captain turned his attention to the soldiers. 'You men will take your orders from *General* Grant.' He flashed a quick smile at that man, before darting out through the door behind them.

The Lakota war party had experienced mixed fortune since beginning their lightning raid on the presidential train. Even though initially aided by the renegade white

99

men, they had been rebuffed at two strongpoints where the bluecoat infantry had managed to congregate with enough firepower. Their chances of actually capturing the whole cursed contraption appeared to be slim, but then their luck changed.

Having shot the soldiers off the roof, a group of warriors dismounted and leapt aboard the carriage containing the kitchen. With great relish they butchered the servants, including the coloured valet who had failed to heed the upstart officer's command to douse the cooking fire. Two of them got around behind the iron range and with a great heave tipped it on its side. Red-hot coals spilled out on to the wooden floor and suddenly the Lakotas had recruited a valuable ally: fire.

Captain Beauchamp tore open the door and came face to face with an elated warrior. They were so close that he could smell the grease and sweat on the Indian's body. Once you've killed it only ever gets easier, so instinctively he stabbed his gun muzzle into the man's naked stomach and squeezed the trigger. The muzzle flash charcoaled the sun-bronzed flesh, even as the ball ploughed through muscle and soft tissue. Thrusting the mortally wounded warrior aside, the young officer immediately recognized that he had a calamitous problem to contend with. The floor around the oven had burst into flames and seemed likely to spread unchecked. The other Indians had retreated to their ponies and were galloping to the rear of the train. They obviously intended to watch from there as the flames consumed the carriages one by one. The surviving soldiers would be left with no option other than to flee and then be hunted down in open country.

CHAPTER TEN

The horses were flagging. They had been driven too hard as a consequence of Thad's iron determination. Twice Jud had suggested that they ease off the pace, but he had been brusquely rebuffed. The troopers' initial enthusiasm for the chase had dwindled. They were beginning to miss even the spartan comforts of Fort Sedgwick. O'Halloran knew that the pace was ruinous and mentioned it to his lieutenant, but that man was too much in awe of the Justice Department investigators to complain.

It was Thad, as the self-appointed point man, who first heard the gunfire. Even over the pounding of many hoofs there was no disputing it. Somewhere up ahead a fight was in progress and Thad would have bet his bottom dollar that the President's train was involved.

'Do you hear that?' he bellowed back down the column. 'You men signed up to fight and by God that's what you're going to do!' He lashed his horse's flanks with the reins, determined to extract every last bit of speed. The prospect of action reinvigorated most of the men and they urged their tired mounts to greater efforts. Thaddeus McEvoy's only thoughts during that last desperate gallop were that they should be in time.

The idea was of such staggering simplicity that Jonas Beauchamp paused to reconsider it in disbelief. If the engine were to pull the train forward until the blazing carriage was parallel with the water tank a deluge could be released on to the flames. Since he didn't realize that the crew had been slaughtered, the only apparent obstacle that remained was the eviction of the gunmen in their cab.

The flames were taking hold on the walls and his mind was made up. The army officer backed out of the carriage, then dropped down next to the track on the side nearest the cabin. He didn't expect to encounter any Indians, so the bullet that slammed into the woodwork took him by surprise. Nelson was still beneath the tank and obeying Dalton's instructions to fire on anyone with a gun.

Spurred on to even greater speed, the captain sprinted past the burning carriage. Even then he could feel the intense heat coming through the walls. Upon reaching the next one he fired once for effect and then leapt up the steps before the hidden gunman could draw a bead on him. As he burst through yet another door, a startled infantryman levelled his Springfield at him.

'As you were, soldier,' Beauchamp barked out, suddenly uncomfortably aware of the torrent of sweat pouring off his face.

He swiftly appraised the situation and realized that the men no longer had any hostiles to shoot at and were standing idle. That was about to change. Whilst reloading the empty chambers of his Colt, he stated his intentions.

'The renegades who killed your comrades could well be in the engine cab. Another of them is certainly under the water tank. We're going to settle matters with them now.'

At his command the ten men split into two equal squads. He savagely kicked the armrest away from the nearest bench seat and, ignoring the bemused glances, took it with him. At the head of one squad Beauchamp led them swiftly down the steps on the left-hand side facing the engine. The Lakotas were swarming around the rear of the train, exchanging shots with Grant's men as they waited for the flames to spread.

Advancing swiftly past the next carriage the six men reached the tender without provoking a reaction. What they did discover was the body of one of the locomotive's crew. It raised doubts in the captain's mind, but by then it was too late. The other squad was working to a count of twenty, so they had to move fast. Taking careful aim, their officer launched the heavy wooden armrest into the cab.

Brett Dalton and Brad Taylor waited patiently in the apparent safety of the cab. So long as the shooting continued there was nothing for them to do. They could let the opposing sides fight their way to extinction. With any luck, the President would take a bullet and save them the job. As time went by the firing seemed to move to the rear of the train, which was a good thing since that was where Grant was likely to be. Nelson fired his rifle, but it seemed to come to nothing and gradually the two gunmen were lulled into a false sense of security.

The heavy object that suddenly crashed down near the firebox took them completely unawares. As Dalton instinctively turned to look, shots rang out from trackside and his companion gave a strangled cry. Pulling back from the entrance, the assassin fired twice with his rifle. Taylor was sprawled over the armrest, bleeding profusely from his belly and quite obviously beyond help. Then shots came from the other side and were returned by Nelson.

It was obvious that the latest group of soldiers knew their business and Dalton was suddenly feeling very exposed. Making a snap decision, he leapt from the engine and ran for the cabin as though the hounds of hell were after him. Bullets kicked up the ground around him and if seven-league boots had existed outside fairy tales he would have given any amount for a pair.

Nelson, now alone under the water tank, bellowed after him, 'Don't leave me, you stinking son of a bitch!'

With soldiers moving in on him from two sides the cadaverous outlaw manically worked the action of his repeating rifle. He sent an advancing bluecoat tumbling to the ground, but then made what proved to be a fatal mistake. Unwisely struggling to his feet to follow his boss, he was struck in the left thigh. Spinning around, the gunhand fell against one of the tank's supports. Then another bullet smashed into the side of his skull and suddenly it was all over.

Thaddeus McEvoy and his Fifth Cavalry detachment wheeled into line and prepared to charge. The Lakotas were wholly occupied with both observing the growing inferno and exchanging rifle fire with the soldiers stationed in the last carriage. Solely military manoeuvres could safely be left to Lieutenant Galloway and that man was glad to regain control of his small force, if only for a short while. Drawing his sword, the young officer gave the necessary commands and the troopers spurred forward. Their horses were almost done in, but even they seemed to sense the excitement.

Thad caught Jud's eye and they both smiled wearily. A cavalry charge was something beyond their experience. They had placed themselves at one end of the line with revolvers drawn and were keeping pace with the troopers. Miraculously their advance was still undiscovered and gradually the exhausted animals increased speed. Under great urging and not a little cruelty, full gallop was eventually reached and the ground seemed to race by. Dust, sweat and aching joints were all forgotten in the sheer exhilaration of the flat-out attack.

'Powder-burn the bastards!' Sergeant O'Halloran bellowed. He, like everyone else, was consumed by the moment. And then, at last, their approach was discovered.

With howls of dismay the Lakota warriors turned to face a totally unexpected foe. A few desultory shots rang out, but as was their way the Indians recognized that their magic had abruptly turned bad and their hearts were suddenly no longer in the fight.

Precariously holding their reins, the troopers managed to unleash a ragged volley. Their accuracy was appalling, but a couple of ponies crashed to the ground and then it was all over. The remaining warriors took off for the hills at speed and Lieutenant Galloway was suddenly a very happy man. After all, his men had saved the President and promotion must surely be guaranteed.

Leaving the troopers to chase off the stragglers Thad and his companion made straight for the rear carriage. His heart sank at the visible destruction. Seemingly every piece of glass was shattered and the polished woodwork was riddled with bullet holes. Could anyone have actually survived that?

The short, stubby figure of President Ulysses S. Grant shuffled over to the platform. Each hand contained a Colt Navy revolver. He was grubby and powder-stained and there was no sign of his customary cigar, but by God he was alive and that was all that mattered.

'I take it that you'll be Mr McEvoy,' came the calm greeting, and for once in his life Thaddeus was quite simply lost for words. Even when he could eventually think of something to say he found that his mouth was dry with dust, so he had to content himself with merely an emotive nod. As the tension drained from the situation, both men exchanged broad smiles. Then, without any warning, the train moved!

Captain Jonas Beauchamp dropped down from the blood-drenched cab and glanced over at the Barklams' cabin. The surviving gun thug had raced off into there, but he would have to keep. There were more important matters to attend to, like saving the train. Flames had by then engulfed the whole carriage and would soon spread. The problem was that, with the crew dead, he knew what to do, but not how to do it. Then, from just beyond the water tower, he spotted a tall man in overalls. That individual appeared to be unarmed and highly agitated.

'You there. Raise your hands and come closer.'

Under the watchful eyes of half a dozen soldiers, Tatum kept his hands by his sides and walked swiftly towards them.

'I'm not your enemy,' he stated harshly. 'My daughter. She's in there with those bastards. You must help me.'

Beauchamp regarded him keenly. 'So you work for the Union Pacific?'

The other man stared at him wide-eyed, as though such a question was irrelevant.

'Damn it, do you work for the railroad?' the officer demanded angrily. 'Answer me, man!'

Tatum nodded reluctantly. He was not unaware of the devastation to the train, but all he could think of was getting Sarah away from the murdering scoundrels in his cabin.

'And you could move the engine?' Beauchamp persisted.

Again Tatum supplied an impatient nod. 'You have to help me rescue Sarah. They have no pity.'

At that moment there was a tremendous burst of cheering from the rear carriage, followed by a ragged fusillade. A line of horsemen was charging towards the train from the direction of Julesburg.

'It's the manure-spreaders, Captain,' yelled one of his infantrymen irreverently. 'Christ, I never thought I'd be glad to see them.'

Beauchamp nodded absent-mindedly as he reached a decision. 'You men, keep watch on that cabin,' he ordered. 'Anyone tries to leave, tell me.' He returned his attention to Tatum, drew in a deep breath and stated his case. 'First things first. You're going to climb up into that cab and pull that burning carriage next to the water tank. Show me how to release the water.'

For the first time the Union Pacific employee displayed real anger. 'Like hell I am. My daughter's in that cabin and you're going to set her free.'

The young officer clenched his teeth. He didn't have time for this. His duty was to the President, first and foremost. Fierce determination showed on his features as he levelled his cocked revolver.

'Whoever's in there is going nowhere for the time being, whereas the President of the United States is in real danger of being burnt to death. So you either do as I say or I'll shoot you where you stand. First one leg, then an arm, then . . . well, you get my drift.'

Beauchamp was aware of some of his men staring at him in horror, but he maintained his deadpan expression and his gun hand never wavered.

At last Tatum emitted a deep sigh and his shoulders slumped a little. 'Very well,' he replied bitterly. 'But if they do anything bad to Sarah, you'll be looking over your shoulder for the rest of your life.' With that, he turned to his right and moved rapidly to trackside of the elevated tank. Once there, he pointed to the collection of ropes and brusquely rattled off a series of instructions. 'Pull that hard to bring down the funnel. That one to release the water and that to shut it off again.'

Without even awaiting a response, the embittered man turned away and made for the cab. He was no engineer, but there was bound to be enough pressure remaining to move the train a short distance and he knew which levers to operate to achieve that.

'But so help me, God,' he swore to himself, 'if anything happens to Sarah, I'll kill that soldier boy!'

Brett Dalton peered through the window at the immobile soldiers before turning his attention to the other two occupants of the cabin. His usually calm and ordered mind was in turmoil. From a promising start his deadly scheme had suffered a sudden disastrous reversal. Unexpectedly strong resistance, coupled with the unforeseen arrival of more bluecoats, had left his future in serious doubt. Even a promising fire on the train was at that moment being effectively doused. All that remained to him was flight and inevitable pursuit.

Sarah Barklam, unaware of just what had taken place, viewed her jailer with mixed emotions. The man was a proven killer and had ordered that she be harshly bound and yet. . . . Unable to tear her eyes from his dark features, she wished that the circumstances could have been different. His arrival on the isolated station had made her realize that her life was actually far from ideal and that she was missing out on so many things. Suddenly apprehensive, the young woman stared up at the gunfighter. What if he just up and left and she never saw him again?

Had she been able to look out of the window Sarah might have realized that such fears were ungrounded. For although the soldiers had not advanced on the cabin they did have their rifles trained on the only door. With their slain comrades lying around them, they did not intend to let anyone leave the building. Dalton fully realized their intentions and knew that Sarah was his only ticket out of there. He also knew that there could be no passengers.

Van Dorn had his right arm in a makeshift sling and was obviously in no condition for hard riding. Mind made up, Dalton strode over to Sarah and gently heaved her to her feet.

'What's the plan, boss?' the other man asked eagerly. 'Are we using this bitch to get out of here?'

Dalton's eyes narrowed slightly. Releasing the girl, he pivoted on his left foot and swung the Winchester with great force.

'No, you stay here,' he stated mildly as the stock

slammed into the side of Van Dorn's head with tremendous power. The man emitted an animal grunt and collapsed on to the floor.

His assailant nodded with satisfaction and turned back to Sarah. Moving towards her, he smiled.

'Don't take this the wrong way, but needs must.' With that, he slung his rifle over his shoulder and wrapped his left arm tightly around her neck. Shock registered on her gentle features as he then drew his Colt and placed the muzzle at the side of her head.

'You won't kill me,' she suddenly blurted out with an impressive display of certainty.

He could feel her soft body up against his and the rapid pulse in her throat. Desire stirred within him as he whispered into her right ear.

'Maybe not, but they don't know that!'

As the captain swung the funnel from side to side the warm water gushed over the blazing carriage and gradually the flames were extinguished. He was only just in time, as the walls of the adjoining carriages were already severely scorched. The heat was so intense that he had to keep a hat in front of his face using a gloved hand. With clouds of steam rising from the wreckage, he became aware of Tatum's eyes boring into him.

'Your fire's out, bluebelly,' that man snarled impatiently. 'Now you've other business to attend to.'

Beauchamp regarded him sympathetically. It was obvious that the railroad man was suffering with unbearable anxiety. 'The man who ran in there. Was he behind all this?'

Tatum was beyond caring about such things and

responded sharply. 'Who gives a shit?' Then, remember-ing that he did actually need the soldiers, he added, 'Yeah, yeah. I guess so. Name of Dalton. He was certainly in charge of the scum that rode in with him. I can't answer for the redskins.'

All firing had ceased at the rear of the train, so Beauchamp knew that it was now his clear duty to rescue the woman and apprehend the gang's ringleader. Sadly, he had a feeling that neither task was going to prove easy.

The cabin door opened smoothly and out stepped two figures. Yet they were so closely intertwined that they could have been one. Miss Barklam was resplendent in her gingham dress, whereas the outlaw behind her was barely visible.

'Hold your fire, men,' the captain commanded.

'Yeah,' responded Dalton coolly. 'You do just as the man says.'

Beauchamp regarded him calculatingly. Suddenly he sensed that he was up against far more than just a simple road agent and that he had to be careful not to lose the initiative.

'You must be Dalton,' he remarked equally calmly.

'*Mister* Dalton to you, soldier boy. Now you listen and listen good. I'm going to whistle us up some horses and then this pretty lady and me are going to mount up and just ride on out of here without a scratch. Savvy?'

The young officer felt anger rising within him and struggled to keep his voice steady. 'The only place that you're going, *Dalton*, is on trial for treason. Then we can work on that rope.'

The assassin tightened his grip on Sarah and offered an exaggerated sigh. 'You just don't listen too good, do you?'

He suddenly dropped his right arm and discharged his revolver into the ground barely an inch from her right foot. With dust and grit coating her shoe, Sarah screamed and flinched, but he retained his vice-like grip on her.

'If this was a card game,' he snarled, 'I'd say that I have the stronger hand.'

The sudden isolated shot brought about the arrival of the two Justice Department men. Leaving President Grant talking with the awestruck Lieutenant Galloway, Thad and Joe ambled curiously over to the group of soldiers. Their searching eyes took in everything. The smouldering ruin that had been a railway carriage. The tense scene by the cabin and the increasingly agitated figure of Tatum Barklam. Carefully, they eased forward until they were level with the captain.

'It's a good job we had nothing to do with that,' remarked Jud drily as he gestured back towards the steaming ashes.

'Ha, it wouldn't do to get a reputation as a firestarter,' his companion responded lightly.

Their banter acted as a safety valve, but merely served to irritate the army officer, who twisted round to look at them. 'And who the hell might you be?' he demanded angrily.

'Quite possibly your next commander,' Thad shot back.

Beauchamp had no time for this. 'My commanding officer is on that train, mister. Now state your business.'

Sighing gently, Thad proffered his gleaming brass shield. As Beauchamp inspected it the lawman spoke quietly and urgently.

'We've been trailing that murderous son of a bitch for some time now. He is a pitiless killer, responsible for the murder of numerous individuals. Whatever he has threatened to do to that girl, I believe that he is quite capable of carrying it out.' He took his first long hard look at the man who had very nearly succeeded in his attempt to assassinate the President.

The intense scrutiny was not lost on Brett Dalton. With the warm gun muzzle back on Sarah's head, he in turn regarded the newcomer. His probing eyes took in the cartridge belt around Thad's waist, denoting a very modern kind of revolver, and he suddenly put two and two together.

'I reckon you'll be some kind of law.'

'Oh, I'm that, all right.'

'You must have held one hell of a grudge against the Double Deuce,' Dalton responded, with reference to the gutted saloon in Julesburg.

'No, only to the scum in it,' Thad retorted sharply.

Dalton suddenly affected boredom with the conversation. 'So, you're on a crusade. Well, no matter. We'll be leaving you now, law dog.' Unexpectedly raising his voice, he called out, 'Baker, get the three best horses round here, pronto.'

The onlookers were suddenly taken aback, as Baker appeared from behind the cabin leading three mounts. Their presence had been completely concealed by the building. Beauchamp looked enquiringly at Thad, who in turn responded swiftly.

'Unless you want her death on your conscience, I advise you to let them ride on out.'

The officer glanced over at Tatum Barklam as he considered his limited options. However desperate that he was to apprehend Dalton, he knew that he couldn't risk

Sarah's life. Finally accepting the inevitable, he commanded, 'You men, no one fires except on my orders.'

Dalton favoured them all with a cold smile of satisfaction and then backed his captive over to the horses. Using the animals as cover, he boosted Sarah up into a saddle and then followed suit. Baker, still sporting a huge bruise on his forehead, also mounted up and the three of them turned away. Riding off at an angle, Dalton ensured that Sarah was between him and the soldiers at all times. His battered crony was not so careful and was about to suffer the consequences.

Without any hesitation, Thad shouldered his Winchester and drew a careful bead on a point between Baker's shoulder blades. Smoothly squeezing the trigger, he watched with satisfaction as the gun thug toppled from his horse. Dalton twisted in the saddle, fierce anger etched across his dark features but, as expected, he did not retaliate.

'I'll see you soon,' Thad called after him.

The army captain was not impressed with the lawman's unilateral action. 'Just what did that achieve?'

Thad's reply was uncompromising. 'Unfinished business. *And* it made that damned assassin realize that my intentions are serious!'

CHAPTER ELEVEN

'Any suggestions, gentlemen?' President Grant had washed most of the powder stains from his skin, but he still wore the bloom of battle. It was as though the infusion of fear and excitement had actually done him good.

The much-abused and battered rear carriage contained five men. Grant was back behind his now upright mahogany desk. Secretary Delano, Captain Beauchamp and the two Justice men completed the group.

Delano wore a decidedly sheepish expression, but it didn't stop him offering advice.

'I believe that we should make for Cheyenne with all haste. There is a company of the Second Cavalry based at Fort D.A. Russell. We might need their help if this was not just an isolated incident.'

There was a few moments silence. In such exalted company the other three men were reluctant to speak out. Then Thad thought *what the hell*, cleared his throat and offered his opinion anyway. 'It is my clear duty to pursue the assassin for as long as it takes.'

Grant favoured him with a sharp glance. 'Your duty is what I say it is, Mr McEvoy, but I take your point and I do have a personal interest in seeing him hop and squeal at the end of a hangman's rope. The question is, where is he headed?'

Before Thad could attempt to answer that, Beauchamp interrupted.

'Pardon me, Mr President, but before we continue I think we ought to invite Mr Barklam to join us. His daughter is a hostage of this hired gun and he is also the only man able to move this train on to Cheyenne. He is filled with anger and anxiety right now, but we very much need his help.'

The President nodded approvingly. 'Well considered, Captain. Let's have him in here.'

A few moments later a very uncomfortable Tatum Barklam stood before them. He was beside himself with worry over Sarah's situation, but could not ignore the fact that he was in the presence of the nation's leader. Grant, recognizing his pain, greeted him warmly, before gesturing to Thad to proceed.

Suddenly all eyes were on the justice agent as he gave his considered view.

'Dalton rode north, but why? There is nothing up there but the Black Hills and that's Indian country. After what has happened here he's going to be mighty unpopular with them for a while. He's also got Miss Barklam in tow, which will make it difficult to live off the land.'

After a quick glance at the anguished father, he added, 'And I don't think that he'd kill her in cold blood. Killing a woman is a sure way to attract mucho trouble out West. And, whatever else this man is, he is not stupid.'

At that point Tatum exhaled a great gust of air, but Thad chose to ignore him. Glancing pointedly at the

President, he continued, 'Dalton's going to assume that since the train survived, then so did you. Given what we know about this man, I think that he actually has the *cojones* to try again. Which means that he is very probably aiming for the same place that we are. Because don't forget, Cheyenne has a population of thousands. He could quite easily remain hidden there. At least for a while.'

'Especially if he arrives there at night,' added Jud, who was keen to contribute something to the debate.

'Then we must get there before him and prepare a reception committee,' Beauchamp urged. 'We can easily outpace him.'

President Grant cleared his throat noisily. He had heard enough. The others all regarded him expectantly because, although not a gifted politician, he had been a skilled tactician in his time.

'We are not in a position just to race on over to Cheyenne. My understanding is that the locomotive needs to take on water.'

He glanced briefly at Tatum and that man nodded agreement.

'The carriage also needs more water on it, otherwise in this heat it could reignite, and we have bodies to bury and wounded to tend to. If this man Dalton gets there first then so be it, but we will do what we must. See to it, gentlemen.'

Under normal circumstances such a presidential command would have ensured that the meeting was over, but Thad hadn't quite finished.

'If you'll forgive me, sir. There's one thing that apparently nobody has considered, yet. And that is . . . who is behind Dalton?' His eyes settled on those of the President as he continued. 'This man is no John Wilkes Booth. He's not an idealist. He's a hired gun working solely for money, which means that somewhere out there is a paymaster.'

Columbus Delano was quick on the uptake. 'So he needs to be taken alive, at least until we get a name from him.'

Young Jud, again keen to make a contribution, had his own advice to offer, which once given was immediately regretted.

'Money might not be the only thing on his mind. After all, he's taken a woman along!'

Why couldn't she take her eyes from him? After all, it appeared that anyone who came into contact with him died a violent death. Her own feelings towards him contained a fair measure of fear and loathing and yet. . . . Never in her life had she encountered anyone quite like him. He seemed to wear a hard shell that was impervious to all morals and human decency and then again. . . . She suddenly remembered the look in his eyes when he saw her in the cabin with blood on her face and despite the heat a shiver ran through her body.

'We'll set down here a spell,' he called over. 'It doesn't look like they are in any all-fired hurry to chase us.'

'It's you they might be chasing, not me,' she spat back. 'I haven't done anything wrong.'

Conscious of his eyes on hers, she clung on to the saddle horn as the horses slowed down. Dalton had her reins in his left hand as he led them over to the sparkling waters of Lodgepole Creek. It occurred to Sarah that their presence there was puzzling in itself. The long stretch of water paralleled the railroad track, which suggested that the gunfighter was not in any haste to distance himself from his bad deeds.

'Everybody's done something wrong at some time,' he responded softly as he helped her down from the saddle. His strong hands encircled her waist and for a brief moment they stood face to face, their bodies lightly touching. With her mind in a whirl, Sarah couldn't think of anything to say to that and so turned away towards the creek.

Only after she had drunk her fill did she speak again. 'Why not just turn me loose? You're free and clear now. You can go anywhere you please.'

Dalton was watering the horses, making sure that they did not drink too much too soon. Being out on the northern plains meant that he could spot anyone approaching from miles away and as a consequence he was just about as relaxed as he ever got. He glanced over at her, taking in the curves of her supple body as she lay on the bank. 'I might still have need of you, Miss Bark . . . lam.'

The strange manner in which he lingered over her surname made Sarah catch her breath. She had not missed the way that he looked at her.

'Besides,' he continued casually, 'it might be that for the first time in my life, I actually enjoy spending time with someone.'

Her heart seemed to miss a beat. This was crazy. Here she was, held hostage by a proven man-killer on the run from the law and he appeared to be trying to sweet-talk her. What possible future could there be in it? Yet she didn't want the moment to end.

'You know absolutely nothing about me,' she

responded quietly.

'I know what I see,' he swiftly replied. 'I don't reckon a bad thought passes through your head, and believe me that's something new for me. If you really set your mind to it, you could maybe change me for the better. That's if you had an urge to save me.'

Dalton could see the confusion working on her features. Part of her wanted to believe him, which was good. Because if he was to stand any chance of finishing the job in Cheyenne he would need all the help that he could get.

As well as three of the President's servants, two Union Pacific employees and twelve infantrymen were killed in the infamous assault on the presidential train. In addition, there were also a further seven soldiers wounded. The unusually high ratio of fatalities was mainly due to the close-range surprise attack carried out by Dalton and Taylor. The supplement of three dead outlaws to the final tally meant that a lot of graves had to be dug that day. Since Tatum Barklam, quite naturally, did not want a graveyard next to his pumping station, they had to be excavated on the far side of the track and that fact would very likely provide a talking point for bored passengers for many years to come.

The wounded Van Dorn was discovered unconscious in the Barklams' cabin. He awoke to find himself manacled to a bench seat in one of the railroad carriages. As his vision cleared he also discovered that two hard-faced strangers were regarding him impassively from the opposite seat. He groaned unhappily. That bastard Dalton had really laid into him.

Thad leaned forward and, using his rifle muzzle,

prodded the unhappy man sharply in his wounded shoulder.

'I'll bet that hurt, didn't it? Well, now that I've got your attention I'm going to tell you something one time only,' he stated through gritted teeth. 'There's a very angry man out yonder, clutching a Henry rifle. He badly wants to finish what his daughter started in that cabin. And you know what? Unless you tell us everything, we're going to let him. Savvy?'

Oh, Van Dorn savvied all right. His head hurt like blazes. His shoulder still had a .44-calibre bullet lodged in it and Brett Dalton had abandoned him without a second thought, to face the nation's retribution. So he'd tell these grim-faced sons of bitches anything that they wanted to know.

'What did you learn from the prisoner?' Grant demanded.

'Not a lot that we didn't already know, Mr President,' Thad responded regretfully. 'According to him, this Dalton is a very dangerous man, which I think we already knew. He had money to hire whoever he wanted and seemed to receive most of his information and instructions by telegraph. He personally made contact with the Lakotas and somehow managed to persuade them to target your train. Oh, and the law in Julesburg was definitely bought.'

'That's something that will certainly need to be attended to,' responded the President ominously.

'Other than that, there wasn't much Van Dorn could tell us. He has no idea whether Dalton has any kind of fall-back position or any cronies in Cheyenne. I think that we should assume that he has and take every precaution. We will need to stop there to take on fuel and water, but I suggest that you remain on the train and under guard for as long as we have to stay there. Any speeches will have to wait until we get to Laramie. That way we reduce. . . .'

Grant's bearded features abruptly hardened and he raised his hand for silence. 'You forget yourself, Mr McEvoy. Don't ever presume to tell me what I must do.'

He stopped for a moment and drew in a deep breath, before continuing in a calmer tone. 'I listened to well-meaning advice in Sydney and we cut and ran. How do you think that looked to the voters? What do you think will happen when the newspapers get hold of it?'

Thad remained silent as he stood rigidly before the President. He felt like a new recruit hauled up before his commanding officer.

'If I am to get re-elected, I must reach out to every voter that I come across. Otherwise it's all over. As I'm sure you must know, Cheyenne is a booming railroad centre and capital of the territory of Wyoming. When the good citizens hear what has befallen me on this hazardous journey, they will be ready for a rousing speech. After that, no one will give a second thought to what happened in Sydney. It'll be up to you and Captain Beauchamp to ensure that no grubby assassin puts a bullet through my skull.'

He stopped to favour Thad with a broad smile. 'After all, two murdered presidents within a decade would not look good at all. Do I make myself clear, young man?'

Oh, Thad was clear, all right. He was clear about what an almost impossible task he faced and he was suddenly very clear about why Attorney-General Williams had smiled so knowingly when he sent his two investigators into the West.

*

The locomotive whistled bravely to announce the departure of the presidential train. In truth, it was by then a very forlorn-looking form of transport. One carriage was a smoking ruin and all the flags and banners were either charred or soot-stained. Windows were smashed and arrows protruded from the sides.

Yet every cloud has a silver lining. With his eye firmly on the publicity, Secretary Delano had ordered that no attempt should be made to clear up the mess. He knew full well that once news of the unsuccessful attack had got around, the President's standing with voters would soar. In a perverse and bloody way, it would probably turn out that Brett Dalton had given Grant's re-election campaign a huge boost, so long as the President survived to reap the benefit.

In the cab Tatum was doubling as the engineer, whilst an unlucky enlisted man served as a fireman. A clutch of fresh burial mounds was there for all to see, as were a number of mounted warriors on the crest of the hill. It occurred to the surviving railroad man that his cabin could well have been destroyed by the time that he returned, but that if he did not find his daughter such a trivial matter would not matter a damn anyhow.

CHAPTER TWELVE

The settlement that the two riders were approaching was known as the Magic City of the Plains and this was not just naïve optimism. Since the arrival of the railroad, the population had grown rapidly to many thousands and a large proportion of it was given over to vice rather than church-going. Even though it was fully dark, Cheyenne was buzzing. The pitch torches that flared in the streets, coupled with the kerosene lamps in the numerous saloons, acted like a massive beacon that could be seen miles away.

Staying close to the track, Brett Dalton and his companion rode into the city from the east. Having kept the rails in sight all afternoon, he knew for a certainty that they had arrived before the presidential train. Grant and his entourage had obviously had plenty to occupy them at Lodgepole Creek. That fact would conveniently allow the hired gun the necessary time to get situated. As they reached the outlying buildings, he reined in to get his bearings. He had passed through Cheyenne only once before, but a man in his profession never forgot a layout.

As was so often the case in railroad towns, the community was effectively split in half by the tracks themselves. In this case the Southside District was, not surprisingly, south of them and contained the huge Union Pacific depot, along with the working-class neighbourhood. To the north lay the commercial district and the all-important Union Pacific land office. Dotted around the whole area lay a vast selection of churches, saloons and brothels.

On their journey across the plains Dalton had been working on a plan. Although Cheyenne had greatly expanded, he still had a good idea of where he needed to be. First stop was the livery stable. Such places never really closed so it was no problem to arrange stabling for their horses. Depending on the outcome of their visit, he might well have need of the animals again, and he couldn't just turn them loose.

Sarah looked on anxiously as Dalton took the stable-hand to one side and explained very graphically how it would behove the man to remain silent about their arrival. After parting with a combination of coins and threats, the assassin was satisfied that any enquiries would be rebuffed, at least for a while. Before leaving, he collected his Winchester and then unbuckled a separate scabbard from the side of his saddle. It was similar in shape to the one that held his Winchester, only longer.

As the two of them left the livery, Dalton suddenly yanked her to one side into deep shadow. Placing a strong hand on her waist, he spoke softly into her ear.

'I need to know if you're coming with me willingly from now on, or whether I need to put your arm up your back.'

Sarah had been pondering over just such a question for most of the journey and had still not reached a decision when they arrived. Now though, as she felt the firm warmth of his grip on her lower abdomen, her mind was suddenly made up. It was undoubtedly contrary to her upbringing and her father's wishes, but she had been taken over by a desire that was just too strong to resist. At the same time she was struck by the awareness that she had spent far too long in the isolation of the pumping station.

'I'll come with you,' she replied decisively. 'So long as you don't treat me like one of your whores.'

He chuckled and gently caressed her flat stomach. 'I don't know who you've been talking to, but you've got the wrong idea about me.' He took her by the hand and led her across the street. The gunfighter knew roughly where he needed to be, but not what he would find when he got there.

It was a warm summer's night and the thoroughfares were teeming with revellers moving from saloon to saloon. Some of the men looked hopefully at Sarah, but then their glances passed on to her companion and they instinctively knew to keep clear. There was something about his features that radiated menace. Cheyenne was a rough, tough city and the people who lived there could recognize trouble in a man.

At the Union Pacific depot there were many sidings sprouting off from the single main line. Dalton kept close to these as he led his now willing companion through the frontier metropolis. For her it was a whole new world. She had occasionally visited the territorial capital, but always with her father and never at night. To her untutored eyes the sights and sounds were unimaginably exciting. They set her pulse racing and all the time she was aware of Dalton's strong fingers intertwined with hers. In turn, that man was very conscious of her change in attitude towards him and the possibilities filled him with anticipation.

Furthermore, if he hadn't been so intent on finding his way, he might well have realized that they were now being followed.

The eyes that viewed their progress didn't belong to some hopeful card-sharp or lustful track worker. Their possessor had seen and done pretty much everything in his life and he knew all about Brett Dalton. The gun-fighter's sudden arrival in Cheyenne undoubtedly meant trouble for somebody and would have to be investigated. Following two linked people was an easy task, so the solitary individual was able to stay well back and remain unobserved.

Ma Bristow's 'Rooms for Rent' was situated at the end of a railway siding and was exactly what Dalton was looking for. Not for him the flash luxury of a prominent hotel. That would have to wait for a time when all business had been attended to.

The lateness of the hour was of no concern to the portly widow, who seized his money with alacrity. As they ascended to the first floor, one of the stairs creaked loudly and he made a mental note as to its position. At the shoo-tist's request, the landlady showed them to a room overlooking the depot, which suited him just fine. She favoured Sarah with a sharp glance, but made no comment before closing the door behind her. The accom-modation had undeniably seen better days, but it was relatively clean and the mattress seemed to be free of ticks.

Before lighting the kerosene lamp he stowed both his Winchester and the heavy scabbard under the bed. Then he moved over to the window and peered through the gloom towards the railroad sidings. When the presidential train eventually steamed in it would require a great deal of repair work and so would in all likelihood be moved on to a siding to keep the main line clear. After such momentous events, Grant would definitely be expected to make a speech, and what better place to do it than on the battered carriage that had brought him there?

A grim smile flickered briefly across Dalton's face as he closed the frayed, unlined curtains. Whatever time the train pulled in, there would be nothing for him to do until daylight. With that in mind he turned and settled his hungry eyes on the delectable young lady who had just happened to cross his path. She was sitting nervously on the bed, as though wondering just what she had let herself in for. With a conscious effort, he relaxed his features and moved slowly over to join her. Very gently, he ran his fingers over the side of her neck. Sarah smiled up at him shyly and he actually felt his heart begin to ache with unexpected emotions. It was the recognition that such things could have no place in his current life that jarringly brought him back to reality. That and the knowledge that the stair hadn't creaked under the landlady's departing feet!

Having placed a forefinger to Sarah's lips, he then moved carefully over to the entrance. He took hold of the handle, violently twisted it and jerked the door open in one fluid movement. There on the landing by the top of the stairs stood Ma Bristow. Light from the single oil lamp flickered on her startled features as she instinctively recoiled. A mixture of fear and guilt crept over her sweaty face as Dalton took a step towards the meddlesome proprietress.

'If you're not careful, you might just fall down those stairs,' he hissed with quiet ferocity.

Her beady eyes settled on his for a brief moment, then she scuttled back down the stairs, attended by a loud creak.

'What did she want?' Sarah enquired anxiously.

'Some folks just have to pry, I guess.' Then he added with a definite air of menace, 'It can be a dangerous pastime, though.'

Dalton quietly closed the door and again settled his gaze on her. 'You know, once this is over I'll be heading south. A long way south, down Mexico way. We could live high down there while the dust settles.' As the hired gun painted his alluring picture, he sat down next to her on the bed and began to caress her neck gently. 'They have no love for Yankee presidents and I'll have plenty of pesos to oil the wheels. Your life could be more than you'd ever dreamed of. As many pretty dresses as you wanted and no more chores. Servants to run your bathwater. Think on that.'

In spite of the situation she found herself responding to his softly spoken entreaties. Having led so sheltered a life, she found that such attention from a mature and dominating man was difficult to resist. Without warning his other hand was suddenly on her right thigh. Now firmly under his spell, she actually welcomed his advances. And then the stair creaked!

'Oh, what now?' he hissed in exasperation.

Then it creaked again and he was off the bed with the speed of a striking snake. He drew his Colt, cocked it inside his jacket to muffle the noise, then dropped to crouch behind the door. Had he been alone, Dalton would have extinguished the lamp, but he knew that Sarah's presence would likely confuse any unwelcome visitors.

Whoever they were, the newcomers knew their business. They approached the door in silence and listened for a few moments before knocking loudly. Sarah jumped nervously and instinctively glanced down at her companion for guidance. Then, on receiving a rapid gesture in response, she called out, 'Who is it?'

After a moment a gruff voice replied, 'I carry the law in this town, lady. Open up.'

Dalton lay flat on the floor with his revolver pointing up at the doorway. He gave a curt nod. The young lady rose up from the bed and walked over to the door. In the tense silence her footsteps sounded abnormally loud on the floorboards. Taking a deep breath, she grasped the handle and opened the door.

Sarah jerked back in surprise at the sight of the figure before her. It wasn't the badge of office on his chest that caused her reaction, or even the presence of another man behind him. The marshal was tall and lean, with greying hair and craggy features. His right hand rested on the butt of a revolver. The deputy peered through the crack between the hinges, searching for any threat. He too grasped a holstered weapon, but none of this had caused her startled reaction. It was the lawman's eyes. They possessed an unsettling intensity that reminded Sarah of her erstwhile kidnapper. So much so that she wordlessly retreated into the room.

'I guess that means you're inviting us in,' drawled the marshal as he followed on. As he went beyond the open door, his eyes darted to the right and he froze. Behind him, the deputy spotted the reaction, but had no way of identifying the threat.

Brett Dalton had his Colt aimed unerringly at the

lawman's torso as he spoke. 'I'm sure you don't need being told to keep that Remington holstered.' Without awaiting a response, he added, 'So, what brings Cheyenne's finest over here at this time of night?'

The marshal remained ice cool and chose to answer a question with a question, which conveniently served as an explanation of his predicament.

'What do you suppose Deputy Thorpe is going to do when he realizes you've got a belt gun on me from behind the door?'

The gunhand was equally unruffled. 'Whatever your man does, you'll take a lead pill. But hey, wouldn't all that be a bit of a waste unless you've got some papers on me? I haven't even broken any laws in Cheyenne . . . yet!'

Dalton's barefaced cheek caused Sarah to catch her breath, which in turn brought the marshal's attention back on to her. His eyes seemed to bore straight into her as he took in her clothes, features and very probably what she had last eaten.

He addressed her. 'You look a little on the clean side for this cold-eyed son of a bitch. Not enough rouge, if you take my meaning. It would be a shame if you came to some harm, miss.'

He returned his attention to the prone gunman. 'I'm going to leave you now, *Brett*, but if I hear of you causing any trouble I'll be back with a mighty big posse!'

The lawman backed slowly out of the room. Whilst his face remained expressionless his eyes seemed to glitter with barely suppressed anger. Somehow, he managed to exude an air of menace even whilst retreating. On going down the stairs, the two men made no attempt to disguise their progress, except that remarkably neither of them landed on the creaking step.

That fact did not escape Dalton as he got to his feet. Nodding his head knowingly, he remarked, 'Ha, that's one tricky bastard!'

As he closed the door, Sarah gazed at him with genuine concern. 'Doesn't it worry you that he recognized you?'

The assassin holstered his revolver before favouring her with a very strange glance. It was a moment before he replied, but what he said took her breath away.

'It's not surprising really, considering that me and that worn-out tin star are actually brothers. Or leastways we had the same mother, which does make us blood kin.'

Tatum Barklam was mentally and physically exhausted. He had never even driven a locomotive before and yet had been called upon to safely transport the President of the United States. On top of that, he was suffering the torments of the damned over the whereabouts of his daughter. Had it just been his imagination or had she appeared just that little bit too cooperative when she had ridden off with the gun thug?

All this anxiety had combined to ensure that it had been a very slow journey to Wyoming's territorial capital. Darkness had long since fallen by the time the battered train was safely ensconced on a siding at Cheyenne's Union Pacific depot. With his whole body drenched in sweat, Tatum dropped down from the cab and made his way back down the side of the carriages. He had done his duty and now he wanted action.

Thaddeus McEvoy and Jonas Beauchamp stood before the scarred mahogany desk and warily regarded their commander-in-chief. Despite the day's ordeal, Grant was seemingly invigorated and in full flow.

'Once the sun comes up, word will soon spread that I have arrived. Everyone will see the Indian damage and the story of our valiant defence will spread like wildfire. So I intend to give the good citizens of Cheyenne a speech they won't forget. A *vote-winning* speech, by God! One that will look good in the papers back East. So if that maniac is still out there, then it's up to you two to stop him. Dismiss, gentlemen.'

Back outside in the gloom the two men ruefully regarded each other. Both were dog-tired and heartily sick of their President's intransigence.

'Doesn't it just make you want to weep,' remarked the justice man. 'God save us from politicians.'

Wearily nodding his agreement, the captain asked, 'So how are we going to play this?'

Thad knew exactly what he intended, but on seeing Tatum approaching he waited until the railroad employee joined them before answering.

'I'm dead on my feet and there's nothing to be gained from getting trigger-happy in the dark. If Dalton is here, he'll have gone to ground. So I'm for some shut-eye and you'd be wise to do the same.'

Glancing pointedly at the army officer, he added, 'Come daybreak, I suggest you do what you're paid to do and guard the train while Jud and I shake up the town.'

Seeing that Tatum was about to argue Thad reached out and jabbed the man sharply in his chest. 'You're about done in, like the rest of us, mister. If you create a ruckus tonight I'll arrest you and put you in irons. Get some sleep and then join us in the morning, but you do exactly what

I tell you, savvy?'

Tatum gazed at him belligerently. He didn't take to being prodded by anyone, but he had the wit to recognize the sense in Thad's words.

'OK, lawman. But I want to be there when you find that kidnapping bastard.'

The arrival of the presidential train had not gone unnoticed in Ma Bristow's boarding house. It had come to a halt about fifty yards from the clapboard building. A rare smile spread over Dalton's hard features as he saw the driver drop down from the wooden cab. The positioning could hardly have been better. It was highly unlikely that the President would leave the train at night. Like all politicians, he would want to gain maximum attention in the morning.

For the assassin there was one thing left to do. Under Sarah's curious gaze he went to the bed and recovered his rifle and the heavy scabbard.

'We're moving. Follow me,' he commanded.

Before she had chance to respond Dalton moved to the door and eased it open. All was quiet. The chastened landlady had retreated to her parlour and the lawmen had gone back to cracking heads. Moving on to the next door, he listened carefully for a few moments. He was conscious of the girl's silent presence behind him. She seemed to be quite good at following instructions.

Apparently satisfied, he tried the handle. Locked. He reached down to his right boot and withdrew the concealed knife. A harsh metallic click and he was in. Together they moved into the room. It was quite obviously clear of possessions and completely empty. Having deposited his weapons under the new bed, Dalton went back to their old room and locked the door. It was only after his return and with the door closed that she uttered one word.

'Why?'

'Because all hell's likely going to break loose tomorrow and I'll need any edge I can get.' He walked over to the window and peered out. They were still facing the train, but the change of room had given him a better angle on the rear carriage.

'That marshal might be my half-brother, but for some reason he takes the law seriously. He knows what I am. If I start anything, it won't matter that I'm kin. He'll come back shooting.'

'And you are going to start something, aren't you?' Her lovely features registered genuine anxiety. She was clearly smitten with him.

Although tired, Dalton felt strangely on edge and knew that sleep would not come easily. He needed something to relax him. Abruptly shrugging out of his jacket, he gently took hold of Sarah and led her over to the bed. She made no attempt at resistance, because in truth she actually welcomed what was about to happen. The beguiling gunman smiled down at her as he began to caress her hair. With time to kill, he honestly knew of no better way to pass it.

CHAPTER THIRTEEN

President Grant lit his first fat cigar of the day and peered through the shattered window with surprisingly eager anticipation. His quality smokes, like his whiskey, were presented to him free of charge by office-seekers and admirers. His gut feeling was that, after the coming day, he would be pretty much assured of another four years of such high living. Early risers were already coming to stare at the battered train and the soldiers were reassuring them that the President had narrowly survived the savage attack and would shortly be giving a speech.

Captain Beauchamp knocked on the carriage door and entered. He clearly had plenty on his mind. His normally immaculate uniform was still dirty and soot-stained, whilst his still youthful features were strained and anxious.

'I've got my men out there, Mr President, but if that son of a bitch Dalton should be hidden somewhere with a buffalo gun. . . . Well, then there won't be a damn thing I can do about it.' He stopped and viewed Grant doubtfully before adding, 'I just thought you should know, sir.'

The President smiled and calmly tapped ash off his cigar. 'Seeing as this could well be the most important day of my re-election campaign, we'd better hope that the newly formed Justice Department is on its toes, then, hadn't we, Captain?'

Rebuffed and back outside once more, the officer gazed glumly around at the suddenly very hostile buildings. Behind any of the timber-framed windows, there could be a steely-eyed assassin lining up his sights. With a mounting sense of frustration, he suddenly caught sight of Tatum Barklam and an idea came to him. That man was walking over to join the two justice men. At West Point Military Academy, Beauchamp had been instructed never to run within sight of enlisted men, but such petty rules were suddenly irrelevant.

Pounding over to the three men, he called out, 'That damned man just won't back down. His stubbornness will surely be the death of him.'

'Well, there's another stubborn man out there and we're going looking for him,' Thad responded.

Beauchamp fixed his gaze on the Union Pacific employee. 'I need you with me. I want you to build up a head of steam in that engine. That way, if there is any shooting we can at least move the train.' Before Tatum could object he placed a hand on his flap holster. 'I will accept no refusal.'

Thad recognized the determination on the soldier's face and grunted. 'You stick with the captain, Tatum. He needs you. And anyhow, you might just stop some lead if you tag along with us.'

As the two lawmen tramped away Sarah's father reluctantly accepted the situation and followed the soldier back to the locomotive. At least there he had some control over events.

'Where to first?' Jud queried as the two men hurried through the awakening city.

Thad was in no doubt. 'When it's new arrivals, the livery's always the best place to start.' Which was where, five minutes later, they ended up.

As befitted a booming settlement like Cheyenne, the livery was a substantial building with most of the many stalls containing an animal. The unmistakable odour of horseflesh and urine filled the air. An overworked stable-hand sullenly regarded their badges of office. He was a misshapen young man with an aversion to any form of authority. He especially didn't like the law.

'You know how many animals come in and out of here every day?' he whined. 'I don't remember half the folks I see.'

'It's a good job that the two we're looking for are in the half that you do remember, then,' replied Thad sharply.

'Huh?' The stable hand gawped at them uncomprehendingly for a moment, before realizing that he was being toyed with. Sudden anger coursed through his veins and he unwisely brandished a pitchfork at the two armed men.

'Tricks with words don't cut it with me, mister,' he snarled in a convincing attempt at intimidation. 'You'd best be on your way.'

Thad spread his hands before him in a placatory fashion and took a step back. 'You shouldn't ought to threaten an officer of the law, young man,' he said. Even as he spoke he abruptly dropped to the ground and kicked out with both feet. His boots crashed into the shins of the stable hand and brought him tumbling to the ground. Before he could recover Jud had swept up the pitchfork and placed the points of the three deadly prongs on to the man's neck. He pressed down just sufficiently to draw blood.

Thad got to his feet and dusted himself down. 'What's your name, son?'

The helpless livery employee stared up at him through tear-filled eyes. 'Joshua,' he mumbled.

'That's a real good biblical name you've got there,' responded the justice man with deceiving good cheer. 'Let's see if you can live up to it by helping us out. We're searching for a man and a woman together. He favours a belly holster and she's pretty enough to make you look at least twice. He may have offered you money or even threats to keep quiet, but now is not the time for that, because one way or another we're going to catch up with him today!'

Joshua stared up at the two grim-faced lawmen and he could feel his bowels turning to slush. His neck was stinging where the prong had drawn blood and he really did believe that they were going to kill him.

'They came in after dark,' he blurted out desperately. 'Stabled two horses. He looked a real mean cuss and one thing struck me as odd. He seemed to have two rifles. A repeater and a long scabbard with something big in it.'

The two justice men exchanged meaningful glances, then Thad nodded. The pitchfork was removed from the young man's neck and thrown off into the hay.

'There, wasn't that easy?' drawled Jud. 'Now remember, Joshua. If we should happen to meet again, you'd be well advised to stick with shovelling shit. It's a whole lot safer.'

The two men strode out of the livery and headed for their next destination.

Sarah woke up suddenly to see the sunlight streaming in past the open curtains. The rays were so bright that they hurt her sleep-fogged eyes. Then she made out Brett's form near the window and the heady memories of the previous night's passion flooded over her. She had never experienced anything like it in her life and the recollection gave her a warm feeling inside. Then the young woman saw what he was doing and all her cosy thoughts fled.

Dalton was turning the old and scratched table into a firing position. He had lifted it back from the window, so that even with it open no one would see him from outside. The Sharps breech-loading rifle had been drawn from its scabbard and was propped up against the only chair in the room. Anyone in his profession would have recognized the Parker Hale telescopic sight attached to the powerful gun. It meant that a man visible on any of the carriage platforms might just as well have been standing in the same room. He was as good as dead.

The realization of Dalton's deadly intentions filled Sarah with dread. How could a man so gentle and tender in the night then so easily return to being a murderous thug? Or was that simply his true nature, and everything else had just been light relief? A dreadful foreboding crept over her at what she was about to be a part of.

'Brett,' she whispered. 'What are you doing?'

That man had just lowered the Sharps falling block and was about to insert a large cartridge into the breech. He turned and flashed her a brief smile. 'Just attending to business, my lovely. You just stay on that bed and keep out of my way now, you hear?'

His matter-of-fact manner stunned her. Hadn't their time together meant anything to him? 'This is madness,' she blurted out. 'What if you do kill the President? What good will it do you and how will you get away?'

A chill came across his features as he regarded her steadily. Patting the powerful rifle, he replied, 'With this, he'll be so close that I could reach out and touch him. One shot is all it'll take and then I'll be gone. They'll be milling around like rats in a trap, trying to work out what to do. Oh, yes,' he added almost as an afterthought. 'And I'll have a great deal of *dinero* coming my way too, because not everybody takes to that Yankee war hero!'

'But what about me?' she wailed.

'Don't you trouble your pretty little self,' he responded glibly, as his eyes wandered hungrily over her naked body. 'Something will turn up.'

Anxiety swiftly turned to embarrassment and she grabbed the sheet and pulled it up to her chin. Somehow everything had changed and she knew that what they had shared the night before could never be recaptured. Dalton shrugged and grunted in amusement before turning dismissively back to his preparations. Some slight adjustments for windage and elevation and all would be ready. At that moment there came a tremendous screech from the steam whistle on the locomotive. The leader of the nation was summoning his citizens, but would soon be receiving far more than he bargained for.

Cheyenne's marshal scrutinized the unfamiliar badges of office. His features remained impassive, which in itself was quite an achievement considering the myriad thoughts that were flashing through his mind. Only a short while before he had received the stunning news that the President of the United States was in *his* town, which, along with the arrival of his half-brother, could only mean trouble.

The veteran lawman decided that his visitors had to be genuine, if only because no one would go to the trouble of making up such a story. Justice Department. Huh, that was a new one!

'So, what can I do for you fellows?' he enquired with remarkable calmness.

Thad looked around the well-worn office, with its impressive gun rack and currently empty cells. Then he moved on to the town marshal and quite blatantly looked him up and down. He took in the lean frame, iron-grey hair and world-weary demeanour. 'It's more a matter of what we can do for you, Marshal. I'd say that you've probably been wearing a badge for a lot of years.'

As the other man didn't contradict him, he carried on: 'So you're not going to want to pass down in history as being the peace officer in charge when Ulysses S. Grant got himself slaughtered in your town.'

The local lawman's eyes narrowed noticeably, but that was the only reaction. Somehow sensing that he was on the right track, Thad ploughed on.

'If you knew of any undesirables who had arrived in town recently, then I guess you'd have to tell me. Because it would be your sworn duty as a lawman.'

As the two men gazed intently at each other, the marshal came to the only decision that he could.

'God damn it to hell!' he exclaimed. 'You don't leave a

man a lot of room, do you? A real mean *hombre* by the name of Brett Dalton rode in last night with some slip of a girl. I know him to be a violent and dangerous man, but unfortunately he's also my only blood kin.'

The two justice men gave out a collective sigh. At that very moment, the locomotive's steam whistle emitted a shrill summons. Grant awaited his audience and time was running out.

Thad could feel the tension building within him. 'And I suppose you'd know where he is as well?'

The marshal nodded. 'Of course. It's my town, or it was until you two federals turned up. The two of them took a room in a low-life boarding house near the rail depot. Real salubrious!'

'Take us there,' Thad demanded. Then, glancing at the gun rack, he added, 'And you'd do well to bring one of those scatterguns along.'

Grant's frock-coat had been well brushed. He had decided that he owed it to himself to look suitably presidential for the citizens of Cheyenne. The parlous state of his carriage displayed well enough what he had been through on the journey to reach them. And the steam whistle, along with word of mouth, had done the trick. A large crowd had congregated around the train. Most of the men had hurriedly pulled on their Sunday best, in honour of the distinguished visitor. Some of the small children even waved flags, as though a party was imminent.

Secretary Delano was keen to get him out there. 'It's a pity they couldn't have got a band together, but no matter. This could be the high point of your campaign, Mr President.'

With those words ringing in his ears, President Grant stepped out on to the carriage platform to rapturous applause. All those present had heard about his miraculous escape from the Sioux, the tales of which had expanded with the telling. They were all touchingly pleased that he had reached the safety of their town.

The three lawmen moved swiftly through the almost deserted streets. It seemed as though the whole town was congregated around the presidential train.

Thad glanced at the marshal and remarked, 'If we're likely going to get shot at, we ought to at least know each other's given name, don't you think?'

The other man stopped abruptly. 'Yeah, I reckon so. The name's Benteen. Clay Benteen.' He proffered his right hand, which was grasped by the two justice men as they in turn introduced themselves.

Thad pondered the suddenly familiar moniker. 'I've heard of you. You reined in the Ritson brothers over in Springfield, Illinois. By all accounts they were two tough sons of bitches. What brought you out here?'

Benteen smiled wryly. 'That's the trouble. Everyone's heard of the Ritson brothers. That kind of reputation can make things hard, so I headed West to start afresh. Problem is, trouble can follow a man around.'

'Meaning Brett Dalton,' Jud remarked.

'Exactly,' was Benteen's deadpan response.

Brett Dalton smiled grimly as the short, bearded figure appeared on the open platform. He closed the breech of the Sharps and drew the butt into his shoulder. His right eye peered through the telescopic sight. One good shot was all that he needed and he suddenly had all the time in the world. Grant quite obviously intended remaining where all the spectators could see him to make his speech, and conveniently it was where he was most vulnerable.

'Look at the stupid son of a bitch,' the assassin muttered half to himself as he pulled back the hammer. 'He must think that frock-coat will ward off bullets.'

Sarah stared at him in abject horror. How could this be happening? During the first attempt on Grant's life she had been held prisoner, whereas now she was apparently a willing onlooker. As the enormity of what was about to happen gripped her, she realized that she couldn't just sit idly by. Desperately, the young woman looked around for a weapon. Something, anything with which to subdue the gunman.

At the side of the bed was a piss-pot containing an unpleasant cocktail of urine passed in the night. It was a clumsy weapon, but it would have to suffice. As Dalton's finger began to tighten on the trigger, Sarah carefully reached down. She took hold of the clay pot and suddenly hurled it at him with all her might. The receptacle shattered on his right shoulder, showering him in bitter fluid at the very moment when he squeezed the trigger. In the enclosed space, the detonation sounded like an artillery round and the room was suddenly filled with acrid smoke.

The .52-calibre bullet smashed into the roof of Grant's carriage. The President was in full flow, explaining why the good folks really should re-elect him. He merely glanced round in annoyance. He had heard plenty of gunfire in the late war, and anyway did not like being interrupted. Dalton, seeing that his target was still in sight, kept calm and moved with frightening speed. Retaining the Sharps in his left hand, he leapt over towards the bed and struck Sarah a savage backhand blow across her face. She screamed in pain and fell back on to the dishevelled sheets.

The gunman moved back to the table and dropped the falling block to eject and replace the spent cartridge. Close the breech, cock the hammer and the weapon would be ready again. Grimacing with distaste, he swiftly used a kerchief to wipe the stinging liquid from his right eye. Remarkably, the President was still on the platform and seemed disinclined to move.

Captain Beauchamp knew exactly what had happened and had no scruples about assaulting a President. Launching himself up the carriage stairs, he threw himself bodily at the short, stubby figure. As another shot rang out the two men tumbled uncontrollably on to the already blood-stained carpet. Screams rang out in the crowd as the massed audience finally realized just what was happening.

Lifting himself off Grant's winded figure, the captain bellowed out to his men, 'Return fire, goddamn it!'

The infantrymen didn't know exactly where the shots had come from, but as the spectators scattered, one of their number pointed at a building near the end of the line. An order was an order, so a number of the soldiers emptied their rifles in that general direction. The ragged volley sparked a panic amongst the thinning crowd. People tripped, children were trampled and the President's unusually rousing speech was completely forgotten.

The three men had made rapid progress through the

empty town.

'How far now?' queried Thad impatiently. At that very moment a muffled gunshot sounded off to their left.

'Dime to a dollar that's over at Ma Bristow's,' shouted the marshal. 'Let's move!'

The two justice men followed close behind as he raced down the nearest alley. All of them realized that they could well be too late to save the President and that retribution was likely to be the only action remaining.

With the entrance to the seedy boarding house suddenly directly opposite them, they cautiously crossed the street. The fleshy proprietress stood in the doorway, a bemused expression plastered over her sweaty features. She had heard the gunshot, but hadn't cared to investigate. There was plenty about her new tenant that made her nervous and if he chose to take pot shots at the crowd it was nothing to do with her.

'Whatever happens, stay downstairs. You hear?' hissed Benteen as the three men barged past her, heading for the stairs.

'No fear of that. That fellow gives me the shits,' came the demure reply.

From above there came a much louder detonation, shortly followed by a fusillade of shots from outside. With elaborate caution, Benteen led the two federal lawmen up the stairs. He pointed out the creaking stair that needed to be avoided.

Just before they reached the landing he hurriedly whispered, 'I know which room they're in. I'll take out the hinges with this scattergun. Just remember, he's got a young woman in there.'

'We'll try our best,' replied Thad grimly. 'But she might

just have to take her chances.'

Together, they eased their way over to the entrance . . . *of the wrong room.* As the marshal lined his shotgun up on the bottom hinge, the two justice men stood to one side with revolvers cocked and ready. With a deafening crash the first barrel discharged. At such close range the whole charge of shot struck home. With his ears ringing painfully Benteen rapidly switched to the top of the door and triggered the second barrel. As the big gun again detonated with awesome fury he kicked out at the suddenly shaky panel. As the three men waited tensely in the sulphurous fog the door toppled forward and hit the floor with a loud thump.

'You'd best stay on the deck, Mr President, or so help me God I'll put you in irons.' Even as he uttered the outlandish threat, Jonas Beauchamp knew that he had quite probably just destroyed his army career, but he was beyond caring. One way or another he was going to settle with that murderous cur.

An enlisted man appeared in the doorway. 'Someone reckons that the assassin is in the building at the end of the track, sir.'

The captain leapt to his feet, and left the carriage on the far side and pounded down the side of the track towards the engine. He was not a religious man, but he prayed fervently for Tatum still to be in the cab. As scattered shots ran out, the officer reached the locomotive.

Peering up, he sighed with relief and bellowed out, 'Get this machine moving, Tatum. We're going to ram that bastard assassin!'

The railroad man gaped at him in astonishment, but

nevertheless complied. After all, he was beginning to get used to taking orders from the military. The captain stared at the clapboard building situated at the end of the spur line. One of the windows on the first floor was wide open and yet, despite the hullabaloo, there wasn't anybody looking out.

'We're going off the track,' he yelled. 'Don't stop for anything!'

The distance was short, but all the massive engine needed was a bit of momentum. Then a shot rang out from the building ahead and a bullet ripped into the woodwork near the captain's head. 'God damn that man, don't he ever give up?'

CHAPTER FOURTEEN

Brett Dalton was struggling to maintain his iron self-control. The fragmented volley of shots from the soldiers had come nowhere near him, but he had twice had Grant in his sights, which normally should have been more than enough. And now, to compound matters, the Union Pacific engineer appeared to have taken leave of his senses. The whole train was accelerating towards the buffers at the end of the line. Then Dalton caught a glimpse of the army officer from the pumping station and suddenly he knew what was intended.

Swiftly, he drew a bead on the cab and fired. He had no idea whether he hit anyone, because at that precise moment there was a tremendous detonation in the corridor. His attention instinctively switched to the most imminent danger. As a killer of men, Dalton knew his weapons and immediately recognized the sound as that of a twelve-gauge shotgun. By divine good luck it had conveniently masked the sound of his third shot.

Again there was a massive discharge followed by a heavy

thump as the bedroom door went down. He knew exactly what that portended. Swiftly, the frustrated assassin reloaded the Sharps and placed it on the table. With a finger on his lips, he gestured for Sarah to keep quiet. She was curled up on the bed with blood running unchecked from her nose, and appeared to be stunned by the turn of events.

With the approaching train completely forgotten, the gunfighter drew his Colt and crept over to the door. He jerked it open and glanced into the corridor. Three armed men, veiled by a cloud of powder smoke, were clustered around the threshold of the room that he had vacated the night before. With a sinking heart, he recognized the ramrod-straight figure of Clay Benteen. Under normal circumstances, he would have dropped them all with consummate ease, but he just could not bring himself to kill his only blood kin still living. That split-second decision sapped his speed. That and the fact that he was up against well-honed professionals.

He got off three shots before there was no one left to aim at. The first .36-calibre ball struck Jud in his belly. Blood gushed forth from the excruciating wound. The second only winged Thad, because that man's reactions were so sharp that he had started moving the very instant that Dalton's door had opened. As Benteen dropped to safety down the stairs the third ball entered Jud's skull, snuffing out his young life. The justice man collapsed to the floor with an agonized expression etched on his features.

Knowing that return fire would follow swiftly, Dalton leapt back into his room and slammed the door. Then, making straight for the bed, he seized Sarah's ankles and dragged her off the double bed like so much rubbish. Then he got down behind it and heaved it into position behind the door. A bullet punched through the timber and carried on out through the open window.

'You'll never take me, law dog,' Dalton bellowed out.

As if to mock his defiance a steam whistle abruptly screeched out and a feeling of pure dread flooded over him. 'Oh sweet Jesus, the train!'

In the cab Tatum Barklam and the captain braced themselves as the massive locomotive with its projecting cowcatcher ploughed through the buffers and off the track. With the iron wheels now moving through earth, the speed dropped off, but not sufficiently to save the poorly built structure. It was as though Ma Bristow's rooming house was struck by a combination of earthquake and tornado. With an awful rending sound the whole clapboard wall gave way under the unstoppable onslaught.

A choking cloud of dust and splinters showered over the cab as the engine thrust on into the building. With timber supports snapping like matchwood, the first floor gave a tremendous shudder. The nearest two rooms were suddenly open to the elements and both Dalton and Sarah were visible. Somehow she remained on the bed, even though it had been thrown to one side as the floorboards snapped in two over the top of the iron boiler. Dalton had instinctively grabbed the Sharps before dropping flat next to the far wall. Most of the train was now off its supporting rails, the earth acting as a drag that finally brought the locomotive to rest inside the building. It was only the support of the huge boiler that prevented the entire rear of Ma Bristow's doomed house from collapsing in on itself.

Inside the cab the two men were miraculously unharmed. The vulnerable smokestack was the only part of the engine to have suffered major damage. It had completely sheared off and ended up in a steaming heap in what had been the rear parlour. Back in the rear carriage, the President had wisely remained on the floor until the train came to a grinding halt. His experience of bloody violence could be traced back to the Mexican War, so his next action came completely naturally. He crawled over to his desk and removed a Navy Colt revolver.

Thad McEvoy knew that the soft lead ball had broken his left arm as it flattened out on impact. The limb was completely useless and the pain excruciating. He yanked his trousers' belt from its loops and managed to hurriedly fashion a sling. In the deep recesses of his mind he knew that the arm might well need amputating, but such thoughts were best kept buried for the time being.

'Benteen,' he yelled hoarsely, 'are you prepared to kill that son of a bitch half-brother of yours?'

Before Benteen could reply there was an earth-shattering crash and the whole building seemed to shift on its flimsy foundations. As the outside wall fell away from the bedroom, Thad raced back into the corridor before turning to view the destruction in sheer amazement. Unlike Dalton, he did not immediately realize what had caused it. With his body awash with pain, he struggled to make sense of the devastation, but then suddenly found the marshal at his side.

'If the same thing has happened behind that door, we may be able to catch Dalton unawares,' remarked Benteen with remarkable presence of mind, as he hurriedly reloaded his scattergun. 'And yes, I am.'

Keeping well apart, the two men approached the closed door. Grimacing from the sudden agony in his shattered arm, Thad kicked out at the handle. As the door swung open two shots crashed out in rapid succession. Both balls slammed into the timber surround, forcing the lawmen to keep out of sight.

In the little that was left of the room Brett Dalton recognized that his options were distinctly limited, but he still hadn't given up on the President. With his Sharps in one hand and the belly gun in the other, he cast a quick glance at Sarah's terrified figure. Smiling sardonically, he remarked, 'We'll have to do this again sometime, my lovely.'

He strode to the edge and nimbly dropped down on to the roof of the cab. A blue-clad figure challenged him from the side of the engine and Dalton swiftly aimed and fired his revolver. The soldier cried out in mortal agony and fell back into the dirt. From inside the cab Jonas Beauchamp drew a bead on the gunman, but then had to duck as Dalton's empty revolver hurtled towards him.

The infantrymen detailed to guard the train were either in it or next to it, so Dalton stayed up top. Displaying exceptional agility, he leapt on to the coal-filled tender and then up on to the nearest carriage roof before the captain could recover. Drawing the revolver from his shoulder rig, the assassin sprinted for the rear of the train. He leapt across the gaps between the carriages and gunned down two more soldiers as he spotted them aiming their rifles at him. His relentless advance appeared to be unstoppable.

*

The two lawmen entered the wrecked bedroom. Thad was beginning to feel shaky, as reaction to his injury set in. He glimpsed Sarah cowering on the bed, but as she was apparently unhurt he swiftly dismissed her from his mind. She was Tatum's problem, not his, and anyhow he had just spotted Dalton.

'Use the scattergun on him,' he urged Benteen. 'Before he drops out of sight.'

The marshal tucked the butt tightly into his shoulder and peered grimly along the shortened barrels of his big gun. His only living relative had just dropped on to the roof of the penultimate carriage. He had mere seconds remaining.

'Do it,' Thad hissed at him desperately.

Hardening his will to the inevitable, Benteen squeezed both triggers at once. He jerked under the vicious recoil and tightly closed his eyes. He was sufficiently practised with the weapon to know that there could only be extreme mental anguish awaiting him when the smoke cleared.

The pattern of shot from the truncated barrels had spread by the time it reached the running man, but enough of it struck flesh and blood to do some real damage. Brett Dalton was only a few feet away from relative safety when the lead pellets tore into him. His back was liberally peppered, part of his right earlobe was torn away and two pellets hit him in the neck. Caught in mid-stride, he stumbled and fell forward. Years of training meant that he kept hold of both weapons, yet that very fact ensured that he crashed on to the roof far more heavily than if he had used his hands to break his fall.

For what seemed like an age, the fugitive was as helpless as a baby, before he finally managed to suck air into his parched lungs. Getting to his knees, he glanced to the side and saw a soldier staring up at him in horror. Without any hesitation, Dalton pointed his revolver at the man's head and fired. Before the young man had hit the ground, his killer was back on his feet and dashing for the end of the carriage roof. His back felt greasy with blood and his head hurt abominably, but he was still in the game.

Columbus Delano heard a thump on the roof behind him. Knowing that there could be no good reason for it, he frantically tried to re-enter the carriage. Unfortunately his portly physique would not respond rapidly enough. A blood-soaked figure dropped down on to the platform next to him and he yelped in alarm. The barrel of Dalton's revolver struck him a glancing blow on the forehead, which brought flashing lights dancing before the politician's eyes.

'Quit your goddamn squealing, Mr Secretary, or I'll put a ball in your fat gut,' growled Dalton. He holstered the Colt and transferred the Sharps to his gun hand. He was conscious that he might only get the one shot at Grant, and so it needed some heft behind it.

Unaccustomed weakness was coming over Dalton as he knocked on and then opened the door to the last carriage. With Delano in front of him, he hoped to sow some small seeds of confusion. Blood loss was taking its toll and he knew that he didn't have long. Thrusting the dazed official forward, the failing gunman crossed the threshold and suddenly found himself in very opulent surroundings. The man whom he had been trying so hard to kill was directly facing him. Grant's right hand held a levelled Colt Navy, but with Delano's ample frame in the way he had no clear shot.

Logic dictated that Dalton should fire immediately, but

professional curiosity and a misplaced sense of showman-
ship delayed what should have been the fatal shot. It was
the President who spoke first.

'So you're Dalton, huh?' he growled around a half-
chewed cigar. 'Somehow I thought you'd be bigger.'

'That didn't stop you,' muttered the assassin through
gritted teeth. Beads of sweat covered his forehead and he
was aware of blood seeping into his boots. He felt faint and
only his iron determination enabled him to remain standing. 'But it looks like your days as President are over.' Calling
on all his remaining strength, Dalton lowered the Sharps.

Unwilling to shoot his own colleague, Grant remained
rooted to the spot and stared calmly at the gaping muzzle.
Death held no surprises for him.

A shot crashed out, but it came from behind the tri-
umphant would-be killer. A hammer blow struck Dalton in
the back. With an agonized groan, he released his grip on
the terrified cabinet member and staggered to one side.
He retained a grip on his powerful rifle, but could no
longer draw a bead on his target. In the doorway, Jonas
Beauchamp cocked his revolver and prepared to fire again.

'Stand down, Captain,' Grant commanded tersely.
Fixing his steely gaze upon the dying gunfighter, the
President asked the only question of relevance.

'Who put up the money?'

With a bloody froth bubbling from his mouth, Brett
Dalton offered the makings of a ghastly smile. 'You go to
hell, Mr President!'

Grant nodded grimly, as though expecting such a
response. 'That's what I expected,' he remarked. 'But it
seems like you'll get there before me.' He squeezed the
trigger.

CHAPTER FIFTEEN

Not for the first time in her dissolute life, Ma Bristow faced financial ruin. The most recent occasion had been in Des Moines, Iowa when a dissatisfied customer had burnt her whorehouse down, but this was entirely different. A Union Pacific locomotive had been quite deliberately steamed into her property and yet all her pleas for compensation had fallen on deaf ears.

'You rented out a room to a wanted man,' responded a totally unsympathetic Clay Benteen.

'Every man I've ever known has been wanted for something,' she declared bitterly.

For Thad McEvoy, Dalton's bloody demise left him with mixed feelings. President Grant's life had been preserved, but at what cost? That Jud Parker had died in the line of duty would be of scant comfort to his widowed mother, and unless Cheyenne's sawbones was uncommonly skilful it was doubtful whether Thad's arm could be saved. Life would be a whole lot tougher for a one-armed lawman, even supposing that he kept his job.

Tatum Barklam had got his lovely daughter back at last. Except was she still lovely or merely a soiled dove?

'I've been such a fool, Pa,' she admitted as she clung on to him beside the derailed train.

It occurred to him that just how big a fool Sarah had been would likely become apparent over the next few months. In the meantime they needed to cadge a ride back to Lodgepole Creek, if there was anything left to return to.

President Ulysses Simpson Grant had been in a strangely pensive mood since dispatching the would-be assassin. He looked out of the carriage window and observed Captain Beauchamp as he detailed men to carry off and bury the slain soldiers. Tecumsah Sherman had been right about him and the young officer would soon be receiving a step up in rank by presidential command. Such a consideration was not enough to lighten his thoughts, however.

'So many good men have died over this and for what? Just to keep a grizzled old soldier alive.'

Secretary Delano, who had made up his mind never to travel out West again, had finally recovered his composure. The blow to the head had left him with a minor wound that he was actually quite proud of, and he was back to doing what he was best at: scheming.

'It wasn't just you they were protecting. It was the office of President of the United States. That's more important than any individual. But for now that just happens to be you, and all this *has* pretty much guaranteed your re-election. I can see the headlines now: *Merciless Assassin Shot Dead by Helpless President.*'

Grant favoured him with a sad smile. 'How can I have been helpless if I managed to kill him?'

Delano refused to be deflated and what he said next

gave his bearded boss plenty of food for thought. 'You'd do well to keep those Navy Colts close at hand, Mr President. After all, we never did find out who was behind that son of a bitch and if he's got plenty of greenbacks left it shouldn't be hard to find himself another shootist.'

And so it came about that Benjamin J. Fisk, practitioner of dentistry and medicine in Cheyenne, received the most distinguished visitor of his career. Thad was sprawled out on Fisk's couch when Grant entered the shabby treatment room. The justice man was heavily dosed with laudanum prior to the sawbones attempting to set his arm, but he had sufficient wit to comprehend the President's words.

'When you recover, Mr McEvoy, you're coming to work for me. It appears that being a politician can be a dangerous pastime, so you'd better look after him, Doctor!'

That worthy frantically nodded his head as he readied the splints. Thad's speech was slurred, but he still managed to offer a token objection.

'The Attorney-General might not want rid of me, Mr President.'

'George Williams will do as he's damn well told,' growled the nation's leader. 'And so will you, Thad McEvoy. I want you watching my back if and when the next hired gun comes looking.'